Charles Dickens'

A Tale of Two Cities

A Theatrical Adaptation

by Mark Fitzgibbons

Baker's Plays
7611 Sunset Blvd.
Los Angeles, CA 90042
bakersplays.com

The action of the play takes place in the courtyard of an English inn and on the balconies, stairways and in the passageways which surround it.

A small assortment of furniture and sculptural pieces are used throughout to fulfill the scenic requirements.

The time is the 1860's.

The audience is attending the *inn's* production of A TALE OF TWO CITIES. (In the original production, the audience was seated within the innyard environment.)

CAST OF PLAYERS

INNKEEPERS/NARRATORS — *(2 females, 2 males. They will be referred to in the script as the King and Queen of England and the King and Queen of France, which are the first of many roles they play as they narrate the story.)*

MR. JARVIS LORRY

JERRY CRUNCHER

LUCIE MANETTE

ERNEST DEFARGE

MADAME DEFARGE

JACQUES I, II, III

MR STRYVER

MR. BARSAD (Solomon)

DR. MANETTE

CHARLES DARNAY

SIDNEY CARTON

MISS PROSS

GASPARD

MARQUIS ST. EVREMONDE

VENGEANCE

LITTLE LUCIE

PEASANTS

The play is performed in three acts.

A TALE OF TWO CITIES received its professional premiere at The Cleveland Play House, Cleveland, Ohio on January 28, 1983 under the direction of William Rhys with the following cast:

Innkeepers/Narrators...... Wayne S. Turney, Carolyn Reed, William Strzempek, Sharor. Bicknell
Mr. Jarvis Lorry.................... Richard Halverson
Jerry Cruncher......................... Marcus Naylor
Lucie Manette .... Tracee Patterson
Ernest Defarge .... James P. Kisicki
Madame Defarge .... Evie McElroy
Jacques 1...................... Gregory M. Del Torto
Jacques 2 .... Allan Byrne
Jacques 3.......................... Norm. Berman
Jacques 4............................. Peter Schiff
Mr. Stryver .... Allen Leatherman
Mr. Barsad........................ Dan Westbrook
Dr. Manette........................ John Buck, Jr.
Charles Darnay .... Morgan Lund
Sidney Carton......................... Si Osborne
Miss Pross......................... Alden Redgrave
Gaspard .... Kelly C. Morgan
Marquis St. Evremonde...................... Paul Lee
Vengeance......................... Cassancra Wolfe
Little Lucie.................. Adrea Lund, Beth Kadlubak
Gaspard's Son .... Todd LaRiche, Shannon James
Citizens of England and France. . . Ladies and Gentlemen of the ensemble

Original Music, Arrangements, Musical Direction
by David Gooding

Set and Lighting by Richard Gould

Costumes by Estelle Painter

Properties — James A. Guy

Stage Manager — Jack Doulin

A TALE OF TWO CITIES was originally produced at
Kent State University, Kent, Ohio on May 16, 1974 with
the following cast:

INNKEEPERS/NARRATORS

POLLY LAW. . . . . Queen of England
PETER HINE. . . . . King of England
MARCI MAULLAR . . . . Queen of France
BILL WHITMAN . . . . King of France

CAST OF PLAYERS

Jarvis Lorry . . . . GEORGE F. BUZA
Jerry Cruncher. . . . . ERIC KORNFELD
Lucie Manette. . . . . BETH FINLEY
Ernest Defarge . . . . JOHN MLINEK
Madame Defarge. . . . . WENDY KRISS
Jacques 1 . . . . JIM CONTI
Jacques 2. . . . . MARK PIERSON
Gaspard. . . . . JOHN MATSIS
Dr. Manette. . . . . TOM FREEBURN
Mr. Stryver. . . . . RICHARD BUNTS
Charles Darnay. . . . . DAVID PRITTIE
Barsad . . . . DAN EZSO
Sydney Carton. . . . . SCOTT STEVENS
Miss Pross . . . . JOAN G. FOGARTY
Jacques 3 . . . . HARRY ZIMMERMAN
Marquis St. Evremonde. . . . . JEFF A. WARD
Vengeance . . . . CHRISTINE B. GARGOLINE
President of Tribunal . . . . COLE FARMER
Little Lucie. JENNY CHANDLER
Peasant Women . . . . JULIE NERO
                                        LAUREN ESCHUK
                                        PATTI WAGNER

INTRODUCTION

A theatrical production of *A Tale of Two Cities* may sound like an expensive proposition, but in fact this script was originally produced on a university campus in 1974 with a production budget of seventy-five dollars; and it wasn't reader's theatre. This adaptation was conceived with a minimal budget in mind. However, what's important is, rather than stifling the development of the adaptation, that seeming restriction was an inspiration.

In the mid-eighteen hundreds, when Charles Dickens was writing *A Tale of Two Cities,* the English inns were experiencing hard times. In an attempt to improve business, inexpensively produced entertainments were presented in the innyards. It should also be noted that Dickens' novels were adapted for the stage even during his lifetime. Therefore, it's not inconceivable that, in an effort to turn a profit, innkeepers may have selected for one of their innyard productions the popular, recently serialized novel — *A Tale of Two Cities.* (Incidentally, the play could not have been set at the time of the French Revolution, for Dickens wrote about those events from a distance. "It was the best of times. It was the worst of times...") And so, the environment of an English innyard in the mid-eighteen hundreds became the setting for this adaptation. It was a theatrical and economical solution to the problem of literally representing the countless locations in this tale of London and Paris. Actually, Dickens suggests this solution in the second chapter of the second book of his novel. "...The Old Bailey (criminal court) was famous as a kind of deadly innyard, from which pale travellers set out continually, in carts and coaches on a violent passage into the other world." However, the setting was not the only device inspired by the limited resources.

Dickens' story calls for a cast of thousands. This adaptation can be produced with considerably less. In order to effectively suggest the crowded galleries at the Old Bailey and at the French Tribunal, the audience for the original production was seated on the balconies, stairs, and lofts (with their legs dangling over the edge) within the innyard environment, just as their counterparts would have been seated in the 1860's. However, it was the introduction of the four Innkeepers, who wisely chose *A Tale of Two Cities* for their innyard production, which significantly reduced the cast size requirement. In their dual roles as the plays narrators and directors, they perform the parts of the story's minor characters. In addition, the Innkeepers/Narrators solved another dilemma faced by the adaptor, which was to preserve as much of the novel's narrative as possible.

I have experienced two productions of this play and I believe that the key to a successful production is to reinforce whenever possible the concept that the Narrators are Innkeepers and the Innkeepers are storytellers and the play's directors. It's not merely because they're first to appear on stage that the four Innkeepers are listed at the top of the "Cast of Players." They are responsible for telling this story. Everyone else, whether it's a Peasant or the individual playing Sidney Carton, is assisting them in their effort. They are friends, neighbors or aspiring thespians, who are anxious to help out.

Regarding the costume "design" for this period play,

the solution was a relatively simple one, when seen through the eyes of those Innkeepers. Without a budget for such things, they no doubt would have approximated or suggested the "look" of the period with clothing or portions of costumes, which they may have found in forgotten trunks or valises stored years earlier at the inn. In 1974, the university theatre costume shop provided a fair assortment of eighteenth and nineteenth century costumes. The absence of an apparent scheme to the costume design worked to our advantage. If they all appeared to have been from exactly the same period, or they all fit exactly right or they appeared to have been designed as a whole, they would have had a jarring effect on the overall concept.

As for the unit setting, the Innkeepers no doubt would have had it a little easier than we did in 1974. However, with the use of existing platforms and wood planking removed from the side of a barn (with the barn owner's permission, of course) the innyard with its balconies, stairs and passageways was effectively suggested. Old wicker chairs discovered in the basement of a university building, which were positioned on the balconies, complimented the informal "loft" seating described above.

When most people think of *A Tale of Two Cities,* they think of the storming of the Bastille. But how could it be effectively yet economically presented on stage? Two weeks before the original opening all that existed of the scene was a page of the text with the typed words "Storming of the Bastille." Blocking of the scene was scheduled for a Saturday afternoon. It was a beautiful warm spring day. I moved rehearsal to a large grassy area on front campus. As we headed outdoors, we took with us a tarpaulin to approximate the indoor playing space. Something happened once we were in the open air. Whether it was the smell of freshly-cut grass or another sign that spring had arrived and the school year was almost over, we all began to dance and play and fall on the soft ground like children. Soon the gray-green tarpaulin became the billowing tricolor flag of the revolution; and ring-around-rosey became the dance of the Revolution — the Farandole. The product of that afternoon, which was documented by a passing staff photographer for the daily campus paper, became the Revolutionary scene as described in this text.

One final comment to directors of this play. I cannot over emphasize the value of putting yourself in the position of the Innkeepers. Ask yourself, "How would they have done it?" And keep in mind, as you make your own choices during the rehearsal period, that no matter how minimal your budget is, you probably have more to spend on your production than the Innkeepers had to spend on theirs.

MF

A TALE OF TWO CITIES

ACT ONE

Scene 1: *Introduction*

After preparing the innyard for their presentation, the four INNKEEPERS dress-up as the Kings and Queens of England and France, wearing makeshift wooden crowns and tricolor sashes. They perform the following scene in a spirit of playfulness.

For the purpose of abbreviation, the INNKEEPERS/NARRATORS will be referred to as K.E. (King of England), Q.E. (Queen of England), K.F. (King of France) and Q.F. (Queen of France).

As the house lights dim, K.F. and Q.E. are seated on stairs D.S.R.

    K.E. It was the best of times.
    Q.E. It was the worst of times.
    K.E. It was the age of wisdom.
    Q.E. It was the age of foolishness.
    K.E. It was the epoch of belief.
    Q.E. It was the epoch of incredulity.
    K.E. It was the spring of hope.

Q.E. It was the winter of despair.

K.E. *(reminiscing)* We had everything before us.

Q.E. We had nothing before us.

K.E. We were all going direct to Heaven.

Q.E. We were all going direct the other way. *(K.F. and Q.F. enter S.L)*

K.F. In short, the period was so much like the present period, that some of its noisiest authorities insisted on its being received in the superlative degree of comparison only. *(referring to K.E.)* There were a King with a large jaw...

Q.F. *(referring to Q.E.)* And a Queen with a *plain* face, on the throne of England. *(She curtsies.)*

Q.E. *(referring to K.F.)* There were a King with a large jaw... *(She curtsies.)*

K.E. *(referring to Q.F.)* And a Queen with a fair face, on the throne of France. *(He bows gallantly. Q.F. flirts with him while Q.E. jealously looks on.)*

K.F. In both countries it was clearer than crystal to the lords of the State that things in general were settled forever.

K.E. But rooted in the woods of France, there were growing trees, already marked by the Woodman, Fate, to come down and be sawn into boards, to make a certain movable framework with a sack and a knife in it. *(K.F. plays with a toy guillotine preset D.S.L, while peasants in the courtyard construct a large framework U.S. that resembles a guillotine. This structure will remain throughout the play serving a variety of functions including that of a doorway.)*

Q.E. On land adjacent to Paris, there were rude carts, snuffed about by pigs, and roosted in by poultry, which the Farmer, Death, had already set apart to be his tumbrils of the Revolution. *(A group of peasants pull a cart into the innyard through a passageway U.S.L. They position it center stage. This cart will be used throughout as a coach, a carriage, tumbril, etc. K.E. and Q.E. begin to cross D.S.C.)*

K.E. But that Farmer...

Q.E. And that Woodman...

K.E. Though they work unceasingly... *(The lintel of the framework, which the peasants have been struggling with, suddenly falls into place with a bang.)*

Q.E. Work silently.

K.E. Forasmuch as to entertain any suspicion that they were awake was to be atheistical and traitorous.

K.F. *(reciprocating K.E. and Q.E. insults)* In England...

Q.F. There was scarcely an amount of order and protection to justify much national boasting. *(Q.F. and K.F. cross to K.E. and Q.E. standing D.S.C.)*

K.F. Daring burglaries by armed men took place in the capital itself every night.

Q.F. The highwayman in the dark was a city tradesman in the light.

K.F. The mail was waylaid by seven robbers, and the guard shot three dead, and then got shot down himself by the other four.

Q.F. After which the mail was robbed in peace.

K.F. And nobody thought any of these occurrences much out of the common way.

K.E. Well, all these things...

K.F. And a thousand like them...

K.E. Came to pass in that dear old year one thousand seven hundred and seventy-five.

Q.E. While the Woodman and the Farmer worked unheeded... *(Peasants in courtyard acknowledge remark.)*

Q.F. *(The two Queens join hands.)* Those two of the large jaw...

K.E. *(All four join hands C.S.)* And those other two of the plain and the fair faces carried their divine right with a high hand. *(All four lift their joined hands high in the air and then bow. After the bow, they all begin to remove their crowns and sashes.)* But what of the myriads of smaller creatures? Well, they are the creatures of this play, forever proceeding along the roads that lay before them.

K.F. And, it was the Dover Road that lay before the first of the persons with whom this history has business.

Scene 2: *Dover Mail*

The two peasants who rolled the cart into the courtyard will be referred to in this scene as Joe and The Coachman. They have transformed the cart, which is positioned C.S., into the Dover coach. This is achieved by removing the sides of the tumbril, revealing a two-sided bench within.

As the lights begin to change, Q.E. and Q.F. assist K.E. and K.F. as they change into heavy woolen capes, which should make the two men indistinguishable. K.E. and K.F. position themselves at the side of coach.

Lights continue to fade until the only visible sources of light are the two lanterns hooked to the sides of the bench on the cart. The light from those lanterns reflect upon the thighs of the travelers and Joe as they pantomime "walking" next to the coach up Shooter's Hill.

Mr. Jarvis Lorry enters unobtrusively from U.S.R., and joins the others at the side of the coach. He begins to walk in place. Like the others, he is heavily clothed.

Q. E. On that November evening as a cold mist settled in, the passengers walked up a hill, not because they relished walking, but because the harness, and the mud, and the mail, were all so heavy that the horses had three times already come to a stop. *(Q. E. and Q. F. exit with crowns and sashes. The travelers cease to pantomime "walking.")*

COACHMAN. *(He is seated on bench at the front of the coach.)* Joe! *(Lights dimly reveal coach and its riders.)*

JOE. Halloa!

COACHMAN. What o'clock do you make it?

JOE. Ten minutes good past eleven.

COACHMAN. And only now atop Shooters!

JOE. What do you say, Tom?

COACHMAN. I say there's somethin' movin' in the brush, Joe! *(He points his gun in the direction of the dark D.S.L corner of the innyard.)* Show yourself or I'll fire. *(At first we hear only a voice coming from a recess in the innyard D.S.L)*

JERRY'S VOICE. Is that the Dover Mail?

COACHMAN. *(frightened)* Never you mind what it is.

JERRY'S VOICE. I want a passenger, if it is.

JOE. What passenger?

JERRY'S VOICE. Mr. Jarvis Lorry.

JOE. Keep where you are. If I make a mistake, it won't be set right in your lifetime. *(He addresses coach passengers.)* Gentleman of the name of Lorry answer straight.

LORRY. *(with quavering voice)* Who wants me?

JERRY'S VOICE. Mr. Lorry?

LORRY. *(peering into the darkness)* Is it Jerry?

JERRY'S VOICE. Yes, Mr. Lorry, its a dispatch sent after you from T. and Company.

LORRY. *(to JOE)* I know this messenger. May he come close? I belong to Tellson's Bank. You must know Tellson's in London. I'm going to Paris on business.

JOE. *(to JERRY)* Come on at a footpace. *(JERRY appears D.S.L. and crosses slowly towards coach C.S. The coach travellers — K.E. and K.F. — move away from LORRY as JERRY approaches. JERRY hands LORRY a written message.)*

LORRY. *(to JOE)* I may read this? *(JOE nods his head affirmatively. LORRY reads note, first to himself, then aloud.)* "Wait at Dover for Mam'selle." *(to JOE and COACHMAN)* You see, not long at all. Jerry, say that my answer was "Recalled to life."

JERRY. That's a blazin' strange answer, too.

LORRY. Deliver that message and they will know that I have received this. *(He turns to board coach and then turns back to JERRY.)* Make the best of your way then. Good night! *(JERRY crosses to a pool of light D.S.L. All passengers board the coach.)*

JOE. Tom?

COACHMAN. Hallo, Joe.

JOE. Did you hear the message?

JERRY. *(speaking to himself)* "Recalled to life?"

COACHMAN. I did Joe.

JERRY. That's a blazin' strange message.

JOE. What did you make of it, Tom?

COACHMAN. Nothing at all, Joe.

JOE. That's a coincidence, for I made the same of it myself.

JERRY. "Recalled!" Bust me if I don't think he'd been a drinkin'! *(Blackout)*

Scene 3: *The Preparation*

The following is delivered in darkness except for a few candles in the windows of the innyard.

Q.F.'s VOICE. A wonderful fact to reflect upon, that every human creature is constituted to be that profound secret and mystery to every other. A solemn consideration, when one enters a great city by night, that every one of those darkly clustered houses encloses its own secret; that every beating heart in the hundreds of thousands of breasts has in some of its imaginings, a secret to the heart nearest it.

K.E.'s VOICE. Mr. Jarvis Lorry! *(Lights bump up. Q.E. and Q.F. are dressed as chambermaids. K.E. is dressed as the concierge of the Royal George Hotel. They are standing at the guillotine doorway U.S.R. welcoming the hotel's new guest, MR. LORRY, who is stepping down from the coach. K.F. narrates from D.S.R.)*

K.F. There was only one traveler left when the mail

arrived at the Royal George Hotel. He was greeted with some flourish of ceremony for a mail journey from London to Dover in winter was an achievement worthy of congratulations.

LORRY. I wish accommodations prepared for a young lady who may come here at any time today. She may ask for Mr. Jarvis Lorry or she may only ask for a gentleman from Tellson's Bank. Please to let me know.

K.E. Yes, sir.

LORRY. There will be a packetboat to France tomorrow?

K.E. Yes, sir. Bed, sir?

LORRY. I shall not go to bed till night; but I want a bedroom.

K.E. And then breakfast, sir? Yes, sir. That way, sir, if you please. *(to the chambermaids — Q.E. and Q.F.)* Show the gentleman to the Dover bedchamber. His valise and hot water to the Dover. Quickly! *(Q.E. and Q.F. exit U.S.R. followed by LORRY. JOE and COACHMAN pull coach offstage through U.S.L. passageway. K.E. positions a small table and two chairs D.S.L. He stands next to the table with a menu in his hand.)*

K.F. The Dover bedchamber was always assigned to a passenger from the coach. Those passengers always arrived heavily wrapped. Therefore, one kind of man was seen to go into the room, but all kinds of men came out of it. *(LORRY re-enters from U.S.R. dressed appropriately for breakfast. He crosses through the guillotine doorway to his table D.S.L. K.E. gives LORRY the menu.)*

K.E. Miss Manette has arrived from London, sir.

LORRY. So soon?

K.E. She would be happy to see the gentleman from Tellson's.

LORRY. Ask her if she would join me, please? *(K.E. exits. To himself)* A matter of business! *(LUCIE MANETTE enters U.S.R. She stands for a moment in the guillotine "doorway." K.F., who has remained in the innyard, takes her hand briefly as she crosses D.S.L. to LORRY. LORRY stands to greet her.)*

LUCIE. Mr. Lorry?

LORRY. Miss Manette. I kiss your hand. Pray sit down. Something to eat? *(He motions for K.F.)*

LUCIE. Thank you, no. *(K.F. turns and exits.)* Sir, I received a letter from the bank informing me that there had been a discovery respecting the small property of my poor father, who died before I was born. The instructions were that I should go to Paris to communicate with a gentleman of the bank, so good as to be dispatched to Paris for that same purpose.

LORRY. Myself.

LUCIE. I asked if I might be escorted on the journey by that gentleman...

LORRY. I shall be more than happy to execute the charge.

LUCIE. Sir, I thank you. I was told that you would explain to me the details of this business.

LORRY. Yes, I... It is very difficult to begin... This matter concerns one of our customers. A French gentleman. A scientific gentleman. A doctor.

LUCIE. Of Paris?

LORRY. Why, yes. Like your father, this gentleman was of repute in Paris. I was at that time in the French House of Tellson's Bank and had the honour of knowing him.

LUCIE. At what time are we speaking, sir?

LORRY. Twenty years ago. He married an English lady and I was one of the trustees.

LUCIE. Are you quite a stranger to me, sir?

LORRY. Miss Manette, I am a man of business. What I have to tell you is merely a matter of business. There is no friendship in it. No particular interest. Nothing like sentiment. Feelings? I have no time for them. I pass my whole life, Miss, in turning an immense pecuniary mangle.

LUCIE. But this is my father's story, sir; and I begin to think that it was you who after my mother's death brought me to England.

LORRY. So far, Miss, this is the story of your regretted father. But if your father had not died when he did ... *(LORRY takes LUCIE's hand to comfort her.)* if he had suddenly and silently disappeared... if he had an enemy who had the power to imprison anyone for any length of time ... then this would be the history of your father.

LUCIE. I entreat you. Tell me more, sir!

LORRY. If this doctor's wife had requested before her death that her child be reared in the belief that her father was dead. Courage, Miss Manette. There has been no discovery of money or property, but this doctor has been found. *(PEASANTS enter innyard and begin to set Paris street scene and Defarge Wine Shop. The cart is wheeled into the innyard. The coach bench has been replaced with wine barrels. PEASANTS position cart C.S. and begin to unload the barrels.)* He is alive. Greatly changed, probably; almost a wreck, possibly, though we will hope for the best. Still, alive. Your father has been taken to the house of an old servant, Monsieur

Ernest Defarge and his wife Terese Defarge living in Paris. *(DEFARGE enters U.S.L and watches the peasants.)* With a fair sea voyage, and a fair land voyage, we will be soon at his dear side. I to identify him and you to restore him to life.

LUCIE. I am going to see his ghost. It will be his ghost, not him.

LORRY. There now! The best and the worst are known to you. Only one thing more. It is best not to mention the subject of the imprisonment. I carry about me not a scrap of writing openly referring to it. My credentials are all comprehended in the one line "Recalled to life."

Scene 4a: *St. Antoines*

The wine barrels roll off the cart creating noise and chaos when they hit the street. The tall joker, GASPARD, paints with a wine-stained rag the word "blood" on the U.S.L wall.

DEFARGE. *(to GASPARD)* Say then my Gaspard, what do you do there? *(GASPARD points to his joke with immense significance.)* Are you a subject for the mad hospital? Why do you write in the public streets? Is there no other place to write such words? *(GASPARD takes a nimble spring upward.)*

Scene 4b: *The Wine Shop*

DEFARGE enters his wine shop which is located S.L. The confines of the shop are established by a counter, a stool on which MADAME DEFARGE is seated and the table at which LORRY and LUCIE MANETTE have remained seated from the previous scene at The Royal George Hotel. JACQUES I and II are also present.)

DEFARGE. *(to MADAME DEFARGE)* The people from the market are so careless. *(MADAME DEFARGE directs DEFARGE's attention to LORRY and LUCIE.)*

JACQUES I. *(to DEFARGE)* How goes it, Jacques? Any wine spilt?

DEFARGE. Almost, Jacques.

JACQUES II. Those miserable beasts wanted a taste of the wine. Is it not so, Jacques?

DEFARGE. Perhaps, Jacques. *(He is distracted by the presence of LORRY and LUCIE; to JACQUES I, II)* Regarding the furnished chamber you wished to see, come! *(DEFARGE, JACQUES I and II cross to wineshop entryway. DEFARGE points to partially covered stairway U.S.L.)* Follow that staircase to the fifth floor. Gentlemen, adieu. *(JACQUES I and II leave wine shop and ascend U.S.L. staircase. LORRY crosses to DEFARGE.)*

LORRY. Might I beg the favour of a word.

DEFARGE. Willingly, sir!

LORRY. *(softly)* "Recalled to life."

DEFARGE. Come with me. *(DEFARGE takes lantern from under counter while LORRY returns to the table to assist LUCIE. DEFARGE, LORRY and LUCIE leave the wine shop and cross to U.S.L. staircase.)*

LORRY. *(to DEFARGE)* He is greatly changed?

DEFARGE. *(at the foot of the staircase)* You shall see. There are many stairs and it is very dark. It is better to begin slowly. *(They begin to ascend the stairs as the lights in the innyard fade out.)*

Scene 4c: *The Shoemaker*

Q.E. *(She stands D.S.L. in a pool of light.)* The staircase was vile indeed to unaccustomed senses. Every little dwelling within the foul nest of the building left its own heap of refuse on its landing. Up this dark shaft of dirt and poison the way laid till at last the top of the staircase was gained. *(The staircase leads to an U.S.C. garret or loft in the innyard. JACQUES I, II escort DR. MANETTE on stage to a shoemaker's bench preset in the garret. DR. MANETTE begins to hammer the leather with his cobbler's tools. DEFARGE, LORRY and LUCIE reach the stairway's top landing.)*

DEFARGE. *(to JACQUES I, II)* Leave us. We have business here. *(JACQUES I, II exit.)*

LORRY. Do you make a show of Monsieur Manette?

DEFARGE. I show him as you have seen, to a chosen few.

LORRY. Who are these few? How do you choose them?

DEFARGE. I choose them as real men, of my name, Jacques, to whom the sight is likely to do good. But enough, you are English. You would not understand

these things. *(He enters garret from landing. To DR.
MANETTE)* Good day!

Dr. Manette. Good day.

Defarge. You are still hard at work, I see? I want to let
in a little more light. You can bear a little more light?

Dr. Manette. I must bear it, if you let it in. *(DEFARGE
opens a shutter on the garret's U.S. wall, while LORRY approaches
DR. MANETTE.)*

Defarge. *(Referring to LORRY, he addresses DR. MANETTE.)*
You have a visitor. Here is Monsieur, who knows a well-
made shoe when he sees one. Show him that shoe you are
working at. Take it, Monsieur. Tell Monsieur what kind
of shoe it is and the maker's name.

Dr. Manette. It is a young lady's walking shoe.

Defarge. And the maker's name?

Dr. Manette. Did you ask me for my name?

Defarge. Assuredly I did.

Dr. Manette. One Hundred and Five, North Tower.

Defarge. Is that all?

Dr. Manette. One Hundred and Five, North Tower.

Lorry. You are not a shoemaker by trade?

Dr. Manette. No! I ... I taught myself. I ask leave to...
(He resumes his work.)

Lorry. Monsieur Manette, do you remember nothing
of me? Look at me. Is there no old banker, no old business, no old time rising in your mind? *(LUCIE crosses to
DR. MANETTE and kneels at his side. DR. reaches for a tool from
the bench. His hand touches LUCIE's arm.)*

Dr. Manette. What is this? You are not the gaoler's
daughter? Who are you? *(DR. MANETTE touches LUCIE's
hair. He removes a small leather pouch from a chain around his*

neck and compares strands of hair in the bag to LUCIE's hair.) My loving wife laid her head upon my shoulder that night when I was summoned out. She had a fear of my going. When I was brought to the North Tower, they found these upon my sleeve. *(to an imaginary guard)* You will leave them? They can never help me to escape. *(to LUCIE)* How can it be? You are too young, too blooming. What is your name, my gentle angel?

LUCIE. Oh, sir, at another time you shall know my name, and of my poor father who is living, and of my mother who is dead, and how I never knew their hard, hard history. *(to LORRY)* If without disturbing him, all could be arranged for our leaving Paris at once.

LORRY. But, consider. Is he fit for the journey?

LUCIE. More fit for that, I think, than to remain in this city so dreadful to him.

DEFARGE. It is true. Doctor Manette is for all reasons best out of France. Shall I hire a carriage and post horses?

LORRY. That's business, and if business is to be done, I had better do it.

LUCIE. Then please leave us alone for a moment. You see how composed he has become. You need not be afraid to leave him with me. *(LORRY and DEFARGE cross stage left. LORRY exits. DEFARGE waits on landing at top of stairs. LUCIE and DR. MANETTE remain alone together in the garret. After a few moments, LUCIE escorts DR. MANETTE to the stairs and then down to the innyard. DEFARGE follows with the shoemaker's bench. JACQUES I, II wheel the cart into the courtyard. It again resembles a coach. A lamplighter walks through the courtyard carrying a single lantern. He attaches the lantern to a rope, which is slung over the lintel of the guillotine doorway. He slowly hoists the lantern to the top of the door frame.)*

Scene 4d: *The Street*

Q. E. *(She appears on S. R. balcony.)* In the street, one clumsy lamp was slung by a rope and pulley. When the lamplighter hoisted it up, a feeble dim wick swung in a sickly manner overhead, as if it were at sea. And indeed, it was at sea, and the ship and the crew were in peril of tempest. For the time was to come when those who watched the lamplighter would conceive the idea of improving on his method by hauling up men instead. *(LORRY enters innyard. DEFARGE puts shoemaker's bench on cart. DR. MANETTE and LUCIE approach coach and prepare to board it.)*

Lorry. *(to DR. MANETTE)* I hope you care to be recalled to life?

Dr. Manette. I can't say. *(Blackout)*

Scene 5a: *Tellson's London*

Lights reveal JERRY CRUNCHER sitting on D.S.R. steps in the innyard, while Q.F. and K.F. stand on the U.S.C. loft.)

Q.F. *(referring to JERRY CRUNCHER)* Outside Tellson's Bank in London...

K.F. Never by any means in it, unless called in...

Q.F. Sat an odd-job man for the bank. He was never absent during business hours, unless of course he was upon an errand.

K.F. His surname was Cruncher, and on the youthful occasion of his baptism, in the church of Hounsditch, he had received the added appellation of Jerry.

Q.F. It was now the year Anno Domini seventeen hundred and eighty.

K.F. Mr. Cruncher himself always spoke of the year of our Lord as Anna Dominoes; apparently under the impression that the Christian era dated from the invention of that popular game, by a lady who had bestowed her name upon it. *(to JERRY)* Porter wanted! *(JERRY stands and looks up at Q.F. and K.F.)* Mr. Lorry is at the Old Bailey, and wishes to have a messenger on hand.

JERRY. Am I to wait in the court, sir?

K.F. Yes, and when you get inside attract Mr. Lorry's attention to show him where you stand.

JERRY. I suppose they'll be trying forgeries this morning.

Q.F. No. Treason!

JERRY. That's hangin', drawin' and quarterin'. Barbarous!

Q.F. Not at all. Speak well of the law. Go along now. *(JERRY begins to climb the D.S.R. stairway to the balcony.)*

K.F. But indeed, at that time, putting to death was a recipe much in vogue. Death is nature's remedy for all things, so why not legislations?

Scene 5b: *A Disappointment*

In the innyard, the Old Bailey courtroom is set up by PEASANTS. MADAME DEFARGE's bar from the wine shop is the judge's bench. It's positioned U.S.L. The defendant, CHARLES DARNAY, stands in the guillotine doorway. A board has been positioned horizontally across the opening at waist height for a hand rest. Additional benches are positioned on stage for the witnesses. Q.F. remains standing in loft.

Q. F. People then paid to see the play at the Old Bailey. At that time, it was a choice illustration of the English precept that whatever is, is right; an aphorism that would be as final as it is lazy. Did it not include the troublesome consequence, that nothing that ever was, was wrong?

Jerry. *(He has reached the top of the S.R. stairway and stands on the balcony next to a PEASANT. He addresses the PEASANT.)* What's on?

Peasant. Nothing yet.

Jerry. What's coming on?

Peasant. The treason case.

Jerry. The quartering one, eh? *(LORRY enters courtyard and sits on bench. JERRY attempts to attract his attention. LORRY spots JERRY on balcony and waves.)*

Peasant. *(referring to LORRY)* What's he got to do with this case?

Jerry. Blest if I know.

Peasant. What have you got to do with it then, if a person may inquire?

Jerry. Blest if I know that either. *(MR. STRYVER is the*

attorney for CHARLES DARNAY. K. E. is the attorney for the state. Both attorneys are seated at tables to the right and to the left of the judge's bench. Q. E. is the judge. She's humorously dressed in wig and robe. SIDNEY CARTON is seated next to STRYVER. BARSAD is in the witness box, which is to the immediate right of judge's bench. LUCIE and DR. MANETTE enter and sit next to LORRY. DR. MANETTE's appearance is vastly improved.)

Q. E. Silence in the court! Charles Darnay had yesterday pleaded not guilty to an indictment denouncing him as a traitor to our serene, illustrious, excellent and so forth, prince, our Lord the King of England, by reason of his having assisted the French King Louis, in his wars against our said serene, illustrious, excellent, and so forth; by coming and going, between the dominions of England and those of the said French Louis. He is accused of traitorously revealing to the said French Louis what forces our said serene, illustrious, excellent, and so forth, had in preparation to send to Canada and North America.

JERRY. *(He points to BARSAD in witness box.)* Who's in the box?

PEASANT. Witness!

JERRY. For which side?

PEASANT. Against!

JERRY. Against what side?

PEASANT. The prisoner's. *(Q. E. pounds her gavel.)*

K. E. My Lord, this prisoner before you, though young in years, is old in the treasonable practices which claims the forfeit of his life. It is certain the prisoner has for some time been in the habit of passing and repassing between France and England on secret business of which he can give no honest account. Providence, however, has put it into the heart of a person who was beyond fear and beyond reproach, to ferret out the nature of the prisoner's schemes. This patriot, Mr. John Barsad, was a friend of the prisoner's, but in an auspicious hour he detected his friend's infamy. This engendered in him a holy determination to examine the prisoner's table drawers and secrete his papers. After which, he resolved to immolate the traitor he could no longer cherish in his bosom, on the sacred altar of his country. My Lord, the evidence of this witness coupled with these documents showing that the prisoner had been furnished with lists of his Majesty's forces, will leave no doubt that he has conveyed this information to hostile powers. For these reasons, my Lord must positively find the prisoner guilty and make an end of him. For Englishmen could never again lay their heads upon their pillows, that they could never tolerate the idea of their wives laying their heads upon their pillows, that they could not endure the notion of their children laying their heads upon their pillows; in short, there never more could be any laying of heads upon pillows at all until the prisoner's head is removed. *(PEASANTS whistle and stomp their feet.)*

Q. E. Mr. Solicitor-General, you may examine the witness.

STRYVER. *(to BARSAD)* Have you ever been a spy yourself?

BARSAD. No! I scorn the base insinuation.

STRYVER. What do you live upon?

BARSAD. My property.

STRYVER. Where is your property?

BARSAD. I don't precisely remember where it is.

STRYVER. Where was it?

BARSAD. No business of anybody's.

STRYVER. Did you inherit it?

BARSAD. Yes, I inherited it.

STRYVER. From whom?

BARSAD. Distant relatives.

STRYVER. Very distant?

BARSAD. Rather.

STRYVER. Ever been in prison?

BARSAD. Certainly not.

STRYVER. Never in debtor's prison?

BARSAD. Come once again.

STRYVER. Never?

BARSAD. Yes.

STRYVER. How many times?

BARSAD. Two or three times.

STRYVER. Not five or six.

BARSAD. Perhaps.

STRYVER. Of what profession?

BARSAD. Gentleman.

STRYVER. Ever been kicked.

BARSAD. Might have been.

STRYVER. Frequently?

BARSAD. No.

STRYVER. Ever kicked downstairs?

BARSAD. Decidedly not; once received a kick on the top of a staircase and fell downstairs of my own accord.

STRYVER. Kicked on that occasion for cheating at dice?

BARSAD. Something to that effect was said by the intoxicated liar. *(PEASANTS laugh.)* But it was not true!

STRYVER. Ever borrow money of the prisoner?

BARSAD. Yes.

STRYVER. Ever pay him?

BARSAD. No.

STRYVER. Was not this intimacy with the prisoner in reality a very slight one, forced upon the prisoner in coaches, inns, and packets?

BARSAD. No!

STRYVER. About these lists, you know no more about them?

BARSAD. No.

STRYVER. You had not procured them yourself, for instance?

BARSAD. No!

STRYVER. Expect to get anything by this evidence?

BARSAD. No.

STRYVER. Not in regular government pay and employment to lay traps?

BARSAD. No! I love my country. I had to give the information.

STRYVER. No further questions your lordship.

Q.E. The witness may step down. *(BARSAD steps down from the witness box.)*

K.E. My Lord, I desire that Mr. Jarvis Lorry be called.

Q.E. Would the individual just now mentioned please take the stand? *(MR. LORRY takes the stand.)*

K.E. Mr. Lorry, you are a clerk at Tellson's bank?

LORRY. Correct.

K.E. Five years ago, in November of the year one

thousand seven hundred and seventy-five, on a certain Friday night, did not business occasion you to travel between London and Dover by coach?

LORRY. It did.

K.E. Were there any other passengers on the Mail?

LORRY. Two.

K.E. Did they alight on the road in the course of the night?

LORRY. They did.

K.E. Mr. Lorry, look upon the prisoner. Does he resemble either of those two passengers?

LORRY. Both were so wrapped up, and the night was so dark, and we were all so reserved, that I cannot undertake to say even that.

K.E. Mr. Lorry, look again upon the prisoner. Supposing him wrapped as those two passengers were, is there anything in his stature to render it unlikely that he was one of them?

LORRY. No.

K.E. You will not swear then, Mr. Lorry, that he was not one of them?

LORRY. No.

K.E. So at least you say he may have been one of them?

LORRY. Yes. Yes! He may have been one of them, just like anyone in this room... *(to K.E.)* Just like you may have been one of them.

K.E. Mr. Lorry, have you seen the prisoner to your *certain* knowledge before?

LORRY. Yes, I have.

K.E. When?

Lorry. I was on the return trip from France a few days afterwards. The prisoner came on board the packet boat which I was on.

K.E. Had you any conversation with the prisoner?

Lorry. No, I did not. It was a very stormy passage. I lay on my sofa almost from shore to shore.

K.E. Were you travelling alone, Mr. Lorry?

Lorry. No. A gentleman and a lady accompanied me. They are present today.

K.E. No further questions, My Lord.

Q.E. Mr. Solicitor-General?

Stryver. No questions your Lordship.

Q.E. The witness may step down. *(LORRY steps down from witness box.)*

K.E. My Lord, I desire that Miss Lucie Manette be called.

Q.E. Would the individual just mentioned please take the stand? *(LUCIE takes the stand.)*

K.E. Miss Manette, look upon the prisoner. Have you seen him before?

Lucie. Yes, sir.

K.E. Where?

Lucie. On board the packet ship just now referred to, sir.

K.E. You are the young lady just now referred to?

Lucie. Oh, most unhappily, I am.

K.E. Just answer the questions put to you. Had you any conversation with the prisoner on that passage across the Channel?

Lucie. Yes, sir.

K.E. Recall it, please.

LUCIE. When the gentleman came on board...

K.E. Do you mean the prisoner?

LUCIE. Yes, my Lord.

K.E. Then say the prisoner.

LUCIE. When the prisoner came on board, he noticed that my father was in a very weak state of health. He expressed great kindness for my father's state, and assisted me in any way he could. That was the manner of our beginning to speak together.

K.E. Had he come on board alone?

LUCIE. No.

K.E. How many were with him?

LUCIE. Two French gentlemen.

K.E. Had they conferred together?

LUCIE. Yes, until the last moment, when it was necessary for the French gentlemen to be landed in their boat.

K.E. Had any papers been handed about among them, similar to these lists?

LUCIE. Some papers had been handed about, but I don't know what papers.

K.E. Now to the prisoner's conversation, Miss Manette.

LUCIE. The prisoner was as open in his confidence with me as he was kind and useful to my father. I hope I may not repay him by doing him harm today.

K.E. Miss Manette, if the prisoner does not perfectly understand that you give the evidence, which it is your duty to give, with great unwillingness, he is the only person present in that condition. Please to go on.

LUCIE. He told me that he was travelling on business

of a delicate and difficult nature which might get people into trouble, and that he was therefore travelling under an assumed name. He said that this business had, within a few days, taken him to France, and might take him backwards and forwards between France and England for a long time to come.

K.E. No further questions my Lord.

Q.E. Mr. Solicitor-General?

STRYVER. No questions your Lordship.

Q.E. The witness may step down. *(LUCIE steps down from the witness box.)*

K.E. My Lord, I deem it necessary as a matter of precaution to call the young lady's father, Doctor Manette.

Q.E. Would the individual just now mentioned please take the stand? *(DR. MANETTE takes the stand.)*

K.E. Dr. Manette, can you identify the prisoner as your fellow passenger on board the packet?

DR. MANETTE. Sir, I can not.

K.E. Is there any particular reason for your being unable to do so?

DR. MANETTE. There is.

K.E. Has it been your misfortune to undergo a long imprisonment, without trial, or even accusation, in your native country?

DR. MANETTE. A long imprisonment.

K.E. Were you newly released on the occasion in question?

DR. MANETTE. They tell me so.

K.E. Have you no remembrance of the occasion?

DR. MANETTE. None. My mind is a blank from a time

when I employed myself in making shoes, to the time when I found myself living in London with my dear daughter here.

K.E. Thank you, Dr. Manette.

Q.E. Mr. Solicitor-General?

STRYVER. No questions, my Lord.

Q.E. The witness may step down. *(Throughout this scene, Q.F. has remained on U.S.C. loft.)*

Q.F. A singular circumstance then arose in the case. The object being to show that the prisoner and an accomplice had taken the Dover Mail on that evening five years before, that they got off the mail in the night and travelled back a dozen miles or more to a garrison and dockyard where they collected important military information. *(K.F. crosses to the witness box.)* A witness was called to identify the prisoner as having been at that precise time in the coffee-room of a hotel in the garrison and dockyard town. *(SIDNEY CARTON passes a note to STRYVER.)*

STRYVER. *(As he stands, he reads CARTON's note. To K.F.)* You say again you are quite sure that it was the prisoner?

K.F. Yes.

STRYVER. And yet it has been determined in the previous testimony of Mr. Lorry, by the Honorable Attorney General, that these men were heavily wrapped. Following my colleague's own line of questioning, are there not a great many people right here in this room with a similar stature to that of the prisoner's? Look well upon that gentleman, my friend, Mr. Sydney Carton, and then look well upon the prisoner. With a wrap and a muffler would they not look very much alike? I would ask the witness whether he would have been so confident if he had seen this illustration of his rashness sooner. *(LUCIE faints.)*

CARTON. Look to that young lady! She's fainted! *(PEASANTS make considerable noise. After a moment, LUCIE is assisted from courtroom by LORRY and DR. MANETTE. Q.E. pounds her gavel.)*

STRYVER. My Lord, let us review Mr. Attorney General's case. His evidence, the *patriot* Barsad. The testimony that he warped and wrested from that young lady, amounting to really nothing, and the result of which we have just witnessed. *(referring to K.F., who is still on stand)* And then this gentleman ... This clearly indicates that the indictments brought against my client rest upon nothing, save that vile character of evidence too often disfiguring these cases.

Q.E. *(to K.E.)* Mr. Attorney General, your evidence having been heard, hath your Lordship anything more to offer in arrest of judgement?

K.E. No, My Lord.

Q.E. In the name of our serene, illustrious, excellent...

Q.E., Q.F., K.E., K.F. And so forth...

Q.E. The accused, Charles Darnay is found not guilty. *(PEASANTS cheer as they begin to clear innyard of courtroom benches.)*

LORRY. *(He crosses hurriedly to S.R. stairway.)* Jerry!

JERRY. *(He is descending S.R. stairway.)* Here, sir.

LORRY. Take this message to Tellson's.

JERRY. What message?

LORRY. "Acquitted."

JERRY. If you'd said "Recalled to life," I'd know what you meant this time. *(JERRY exits.)*

Scene 5c: *Congratulatory*

LUCIE and DR. MANETTE re-enter D.S.L. DARNAY crosses toward them.

DARNAY. *(to LUCIE)* I am deeply sorry to have been the cause of this lady's agitation. *(He kisses her hand.)*

STRYVER. *(He crosses D.S. to LUCIE, DR. MANETTE and DARNAY.)* I am glad to have brought you off with honour, Mr. Darnay. It was an infamous prosecution, but not the less likely to succeed.

DARNAY. I'm obliged to you for life.

STRYVER. I have done my best for you, Mr. Darnay; and my best is as good as another man's.

LORRY. *(He joins the others D.S.L.)* Much better. *(He shakes DARNAY's hand.)*

STRYVER. You think so? Well, you are a man of business. You ought to know.

LORRY. And as such, I will appeal to Dr. Manette to break up this conference and order us all to our homes. Miss Lucie looks tired. Mr. Darnay has had a terrible day. We are worn out.

STRYVER. Speak for yourself, Mr. Lorry. I have a night's work yet to do.

LORRY. I do speak for myself. Miss Lucie, do I not

speak for us all?

Lucie. Shall we go home, Father?

Dr. Manette. Yes, my dear. *(LUCIE, DR. MANETTE, and LORRY exit followed by STRYVER. DARNAY glances back at guillotine doorway, which is all that remains in the innyard. He turns to exit S.L. CARTON appears in guillotine doorway. DARNAY turns to have another look.)*

Carton. Well, Mr. Darnay, it is a strange chance that throws you and me together. This must be a strange night for you, standing alone here with your counterpart?

Darnay. I hardly seem yet to belong to this world again.

Carton. It's not so long since you were pretty far advanced on your way to another. You speak faintly.

Darnay. I begin to think I am faint.

Carton. Then why the devil don't you dine? Come!

Scene 5d: *Fleet Street*

CARTON leads DARNAY D.S.R., where PEASANTS position a table and two chairs. CARTON and DARNAY sit.

Carton. Do you feel yet that you belong to this terrestrial scheme again, Mr. Darnay?

Darnay. I am rightfully confused regarding time and place; but I am so far mended as to feel that.

Carton. It must be an immense satisfaction. As for

me, the greatest desire I have is to forget that I belong to it. There is not much good in it for me, except wine like this, nor am I much good for it. So we are not much alike in that particular. Indeed, I begin to think we are not much alike in any particular, you and I. Why don't you give your toast, Mr. Darnay?

DARNAY. What toast?

CARTON. Why it's on the tip of your tongue. It ought to be, it must be, I'll swear it's there.

DARNAY. Miss Manette, then.

CARTON. Miss Manette, then! That's a fair young lady to be pitied by!

DARNAY. Yes.

CARTON. How does it feel? Is it worth being tried for one's life to be the object of such sympathy and compassion?

DARNAY. I must thank you for your assistance today.

CARTON. I neither want any thanks, nor merit any. In the first place, it was nothing. In the second place, I don't know why I did it. Mr. Darnay, let me ask you a question.

DARNAY. Willingly.

CARTON. Do you think I particularly like you?

DARNAY. Really, Mr. Carton. I have not asked myself the question.

CARTON. Then ask yourself the question now.

DARNAY. You have acted as if you do; but I don't think you do.

CARTON. I don't think I do either. I begin to have a very good opinion of your understanding.

DARNAY. Nevertheless, there is nothing in that, I hope,

to prevent our parting without ill-blood.

CARTON. Nothing in life! A last word, Mr. Darnay: you think I am drunk?

DARNAY. I think you have been drinking, Mr. Carton.

CARTON. Think! You know I have been drinking.

DARNAY. Since I must say so, I know it.

CARTON. Then you shall likewise know why. I am a disappointed drudge, sir. I care for no man on earth, and no man on earth cares for me.

DARNAY. Much to be regretted. You might have used your talents better. *(He stands.)*

CARTON. Maybe so, Mr. Darnay; but maybe not. Don't let your sober face elate you, you don't know what it may come to. *(DARNAY exits U.S.L.)* Good night! *(to himself)* Do you particularly like the man? Why should you particularly like a man who resembles you? There is nothing in you to like. A good reason for taking to a man, that he shows you what you have fallen away from and what you might have been! Change places with him, and would you have been looked at by those blue eyes as he was, and commiserated by that agitated face as he was? Come on, and have it out in plain words! You hate the fellow. *(He takes another drink, rests his head on the table and falls asleep. Fast fade out.)*

Scene 6: *The Jackal*

During the blackout, the same table is dressed with items appro-

priate for STRYVER's desk — books, pens, tablecloth, etc. As the scene changes, CARTON is still resting his head on the table. STRYVER enters D.S.R. with a basin of water and towel.

STRYVER. You have had your bottle, I perceive, Sydney.

CARTON. Two tonight, I think. I have been dining with today's client; or rather drinking, it's all one.

STRYVER. That was a rare point that you brought to bear upon the identification. How did you come by it?

CARTON. I thought he was rather a handsome fellow, and thought I should have been much the same sort of fellow if I had had any luck.

STRYVER. *(laughing)* You and your luck, Sydney! Let's get to work, shall we?

CARTON. *(After steeping the towel in the basin of water, he places it on his head in a hideous manner.)* Now I am ready!

STRYVER. Not much boiling down to be done tonight.

CARTON. Give me the worst first.

STRYVER. There they are, Sydney. Fire away! *(They begin to work. SYDNEY sinks back in his chair. They occasionally exchange papers. Q.F., dressed as Stryver's housemaid, appears in the innyard's peripheral shadows.)*

Q.F. Sydney Carton was Stryver's great ally. Stryver never had a case in hand that Carton wasn't there. It had once been noted at the Bar, that while Mr. Stryver was glib and unscrupulous, he lacked that faculty of extracting the essence from a heap of statements, which is among the most necessary of the advocate's accomplishments. But a remarkable improvement came upon him. The more business he got, the greater his power seemed to grow of getting at the pith and marrow. However late at night he sat carousing with Sydney Carton, he always had the essential points at his fingers' ends in the morning. At last, it began to get about, that although Sydney Carton would never be a lion, he was an amazingly good jackal.

STRYVER. You were very sound in the matter of those crown witnesses today.

CARTON. I always am sound, am I not?

STRYVER. I don't gainsay it. What has roughened your temper? Put some brandy to it and smooth it again. Your behavior this evening reminds me of the Sydney Carton of Old Shrewsbury School. The old seesaw Sydney. Up one minute and down the next; now in spirit and now in despondency!

CARTON. Ah, yes! The same Sydney, with the same luck. Even then I did exercises for other boys and seldom did my own.

STRYVER. And why not?

CARTON. God knows. It was my way, I suppose.

STRYVER. Carton, your way is, and always was, a lame way. You summon no energy and purpose. Look at me.

CARTON. Oh botheration! Don't you be moral.

STRYVER. How have I done what I have done? How do I do what I do?

CARTON. Partly through paying me to help you, I suppose. You were always in the front rank, and I was always behind.

STRYVER. I had to get into the front rank. I was not born there, was I?

CARTON. I was not present at the ceremony, but my opinion is that you were. Before Shrewsbury, and at Shrewsbury, and ever since Shrewsbury, you have fallen into your rank, and I have fallen into mine.

STRYVER. And whose fault was that?

CARTON. Upon my soul, I am not sure that it was not yours. But it is a gloomy thing to talk about one's own past, with the day breaking. Turn me in some other direction before I go.

STRYVER. Well then! Pledge me to the pretty witness. Are you turned in a pleasant direction?

CARTON. Pretty witness. I have had enough of witnesses today, who is your pretty witness?

STRYVER. The picturesque doctor's daughter, Miss Manette.

CARTON. She pretty?

STRYVER. Is she not? Why, man alive, she was the admiration of the whole court.

CARTON. Rot the admiration of the whole court! Who made the Old Bailey a judge of beauty? She was a golden-haired doll.

STRYVER. Do you know, I rather thought, at the time, that you sympathized with the "golden-haired doll," and were quick to see what happened to her!

CARTON. I'll pledge you that, but I deny the beauty. I'll have no more drink; I'll get to bed. Good night! *(He stands and begins to exit.)*

STRYVER. Good day! *(CARTON crosses U.S.L. Lights fade out on STRYVER's table D.S.R. The early morning light, pouring through the U.S.L. passageway, first silhouettes CARTON, then consumes him as he exits in its direction.)*

Q. F. Sadly, sadly, the sun rose. It rose upon no sadder sight than the man of good abilities and good emotions, incapable of their directed exercises, incapable of his own help and his own happiness, sensible of the blight on him, and yet resigning himself to let it eat him away. *(Blackout)*

ACT TWO

Scene 1a: *Hundreds of People*

The following scene takes place in the Manette's parlor. However, as the scene begins, the only furniture in the innyard is the shoemaker's bench D.S.L. The guillotine doorway serves as the Manette's front door. Q.F. enters innyard carrying a small candelabra with one candle lit. She blows that candle out. Simultaneously, house lights black out; stage lights bump up.

Q.F. The waves of four months had since rolled over that trial for treason. On the afternoon of a certain fine Sunday, Mr. Jarvis Lorry was on his way to visit with Doctor Manette. Mr. Lorry had become the Doctor's friend, and the Manette's home on that quiet street corner in London was the sunny part of Mr. Lorry's life. *(LORRY appears at doorway. He knocks on framework. Q.F. crosses to doorway.)*

LORRY. *(to Q.F.)* Doctor Manette at home?

Q.F. Expected home.

LORRY. Miss Lucie at home?

Q.F. Expected home.

LORRY. Miss Pross at home?

Q.F. Possibly at home, but it is certainly impossible for a handmaid to anticipate intentions of Miss Pross.

LORRY. Well, as I am at home myself... *(He crosses*

through guillotine doorway, passes Q.F. and stops D.S.L. to look at cobbler's bench.)

Q.F. The Doctor occupied this large still house with his daughter and her long-time nursemaid, Miss Pross. He received patients here who had heard of his old reputation as a physician. This brought him into moderate request and earned for him as much as they all needed.

LORRY. I wonder that he keeps that reminder of his suffering about him!

MISS PROSS. *(She enters D.S.L.)* And why wonder at that?

LORRY. I should have thought...

MISS PROSS. Pooh! You'd have thought! How do you do today?

LORRY. I am pretty well, I thank you, and how are you, Miss Pross?

MISS PROSS. I am very much put out about my Luciebird.

LORRY. May I ask the cause?

MISS PROSS. I don't want dozens of people who are not at all worthy of my Ladybird to come here looking after her.

LORRY. Do dozens come for that purpose?

MISS PROSS. Hundreds!

LORRY. Dear me!

MISS PROSS. There never was, nor will be, but one man worthy of Ladybird, and that was my brother Solomon.

LORRY. Indeed! Let me ask you — does the Doctor, in talking with Lucie, never yet refer to the shoemaking time?

Miss Pross. Never. But I don't say he don't refer to it within himself.

Lorry. Do you imagine....

Miss Pross. Never imagine anything — have no imagination at all.

Lorry. I stand corrected. Do you suppose — you go so far as to suppose?

Miss Pross. Now and then.

Lorry. Do you suppose that Doctor Manette has any theory of his own, relative to his oppression?

Miss Pross. I don't suppose anything about it but what Ladybird tells me.

Lorry. And that is?

Miss Pross. That she thinks he has. To the best of my understanding, he is afraid of the whole subject.

Lorry. Afraid?

Miss Pross. It's plain enough, I should think. It's a dreadful remembrance. Besides that, his loss of himself grew out of it. Not knowing how he lost himself, or how he recovered, he may never feel certain of not losing himself again. And that alone would make the subject unpleasant, I should think.

Lorry. True. Yet is it good for Doctor Manette to have that suppression always shut up within him?

Miss Pross. Can't be helped. Touch that string and he instantly changes for the worse. Sometimes he gets up in the dead of night and will be heard walking up and down in his room. She hurries to him, and they go on together walking up and down. But he never says a word of the true reason for his restlessness, and she finds it best not to hint at it.

Q. F. This street corner was often mentioned as a wonderful corner for echoes. And it began to echo resoundingly to the tread of coming feet.

Miss Pross. Here they are now! We shall have hundreds of people pretty soon! *(She exits U.S.L. PEASANTS set the scene with a few essential furniture pieces — two wicker chairs, a bench and a sideboard, while LORRY stands D.S.L. at the cobbler's bench.)*

Q. F. It was such a curious corner in its acoustical properties. Not only would the echoes die away, as though the steps had gone; but echoes of other steps that never came would be heard in their stead, and would die away when they seemed close at hand. *(PEASANTS exit. LUCIE and DR. MANETTE enter U.S.L. through doorway. LORRY greets them. Q.F. places candelabra on sideboard U.S.C.)* The hundreds of people did not present themselves. Mr. Darnay presented himself, but he was only one. *(DARNAY enters U.S.R. Q.F. lights one of the candles. All greet him. MISS PROSS enters U.S.L. with tea service.)*

Miss Pross. Tea time! *(Upon seeing DARNAY, she exits abruptly. Everyone sits down.)*

Darnay. Pray, Doctor Manette, have you seen much of the Tower of London?

Dr. Manette. Lucie and I have been there, but only casually.

Darnay. I came by there this afternoon. I have been there, as you may all remember, before. And I was not in a position that allowed one to see much of it. But they told me a curious thing when I was there.

Lucie. What was that?

Darnay. In making some alterations, the workmen

came upon an old dungeon where the inner walls were covered with carvings by the prisoners — dates, names, complaints, prayers. Upon a corner stone, one prisoner had carved three letters: D period, I period, C period. Close examination found the last letter to be G. At length, it was suggested that the letters were not initials but the complete word — DIG. In the earth beneath the stone, were found the ashes of a paper. What the unknown prisoner had written will never be read. But isn't it fascinating that he had written something and hidden it away to keep it from the gaoler. *(DR. MANETTE appears shakened. There is the sound of distant thunder. He stands and moves away from his chair.)*

LUCIE. Father, you are ill?

DR. MANETTE. No, my dear, not ill. The thunder startled me. It is beginning to rain. It comes slowly... *(CARTON enters U.S.R. and stands in doorway. Q.F. lights another candle.)*

CARTON. But it comes surely. *(He brushes rain drops from his coat.)* There was a great hurry in the streets. Echoes of footsteps coming and going.

Scene 1b: *Crowd*

DARNAY. A multitude of people, and yet a solitude!

LUCIE. Is it not impressive, Mr. Darnay? *(During the following line, all of the other characters in the play quietly enter and stand in the shadows on the stairways and balconies in the innyard.)* Oh, it will seem nothing to you, but sometimes I have sat alone in the evening, listening to those echoes, until they would seem to be in the room. I have made them out to be the echoes of all the footsteps that will come into our lives.

CARTON. There is a great crowd coming one day into our lives, if that be so.

DARNAY. Are those footsteps destined to come to all of our lives, Miss Manette?

LUCIE. I don't know, Mr. Darnay; I told you it was a foolish fancy. But I have imagined them the footsteps of the people who are to come into my life, and my father's.

CARTON. *(He stands and crosses U.S. to sideboard.)* I take them into mine! There is a great crowd bearing down upon us, Miss Manette. I hear them! They come, fast, fierce and furious. *(As CARTON speaks the word "furious," the only character not on stage, the MARQUIS, enters U.S.R. He crosses quickly to the center of the innyard. There is a pause. CARTON blows out the candles on the sideboard. Blackout)*

Scene 2a: *Monseigneur in the Country*

During the closing moments of the previous scene, JACQUES I, II and two PEASANTS join the others in the innyard. However, they are made-up in white-face and dressed in white night shirts and caps. In the following scene, they position themselves like statues on the stoops and stairways around the innyard. They are the "stone-

faces" on the landscaped lawns of the Chateau of Monsieur the Marquis in France. The K.E. is dressed whimsically as the Marquis' valet. He sits at the head of a long table C.S. with his feet upon it.

K.E. On the Paris countryside sat a heavy mass of building — the Chateau of Monsieur the Marquis Evremonde. It was a stony business with heavy stone balustrades, and stone urns, and stone faces of men staring blindly at their surroundings. It all appeared as if the Gorgon's head had surveyed the landscape when the Chateau was finished two centuries before. *(The MARQUIS enters the innyard and stands behind the chair occupied by K.E. MARQUIS clears his throat. K.E. leaps from chair and faces him.)*

MARQUIS. Has my nephew arrived from England?

K.E. Monseigneur, not yet. *(A PEASANT WOMAN enters U.S.L.)*

PEASANT WOMAN. *(to MARQUIS)* Monseigneur, a petition.

MARQUIS. What is it? Always petitions!

WOMAN. Monseigneur. My husband, the forester.

MARQUIS. What of your husband? Always the same with you people. He cannot pay something?

WOMAN. He has paid all. He is dead.

MARQUIS. Well! He is quiet. Can I restore him?

WOMAN. Alas, no, Monseigneur! But he lies yonder, under a heap of grass.

MARQUIS. Again, well?

WOMAN. Monseigneur, my petition is that a morsel of wood be placed over him to show where he lies. *(MAR-*

QUIS motions to K.E. to remove the woman.) Otherwise, the place will be quickly forgotten. It will never be found when I am dead of the same disease... *(She is taken from the room. MARQUIS spots JACQUES III D.S.L.)*

MARQUIS. *(to JACQUES III)* You there! My carriage passed you on the road today.

JACQUES III. Monseigneur, it is true. I had the honour of being passed on the road.

MARQUIS. What did you look at?

JACQUES III. I looked at the man who rode under your carriage.

MARQUIS. What man?

JACQUES III. Monseigneur, of all the days of my life, I never saw him. He was whiter than the miller, white as a spectre, tall as a spectre.

MARQUIS. To see a thief accompanying my carriage and not open that great mouth of yours. *(K.E. re-enters. To K.E.)* Remove this creature.

K.E. Yes, Monsieur. Monsieur, your nephew has arrived.

MARQUIS. Please to show him in.

Scene 2b: *The Nephew*

K.E. begins to exit with JACQUES III. DARNAY enters through the same passageway. K.E. announces DARNAY's entrance.

K.E. Monsieur Charles Darnay Evremonde! *(He exits*

with JACQUES III.)

MARQUIS. Nephew.

DARNAY. Sir. *(MARQUIS directs DARNAY to the chair at the other end of the long table.)*

MARQUIS. You have been a long time coming.

DARNAY. On the contrary, I come direct.

MARQUIS. Pardon me! I mean, not a long time on the journey; a long time intending the journey.

DARNAY. I have been detained by various business.

MARQUIS. Without doubt.

DARNAY. Sir, the subject of that business has been the freedom of France. And I have come back to seek your assistance.

MARQUIS. My assistance, nephew? You will forever seek it in vain, be assured.

DARNAY. This business has carried me into great and unexpected peril, but it is a sacred object, which I will continue with or without your assistance; and if it carries me to death, I hope it will sustain me.

MARQUIS. Not to death. It is not necessary to say to death.

DARNAY. Indeed, sir, if it carries me to the brink of death, you would not care to see it stop there. For all I know, you may have helped the suspicious circumstances that surrounded my trial in England.

MARQUIS. No, no, no!

DARNAY. In effect, sir, I believe it to be at once your bad misfortune, and my good fortune, that has kept me out of a prison here in France.

MARQUIS. I do not quite understand. Dare I ask you to explain?

DARNAY. I believe that if you were not in disgrace with the court, a letter de cachet would have sent me to some fortress indefinitely.

MARQUIS. It is possible. For the honour of the family, I could resolve to inconvenience even you. But I am, as you say, at a disadvantage. These gentle aids to the power and honour of the families are sought by so many now, and granted to so few. Our ancestors held the right of life and death over the surrounding vulgar. From this room, many such dogs have been taken out to be hanged.

DARNAY. We must make amends to these people. I believe our name to be more detested than any name in France.

MARQUIS. Let us hope so. Detestation of the high is the involuntary homage of the low. But you must be fatigued. Shall we terminate our conference for the night?

DARNAY. A moment more.

MARQUIS. An hour, if you please.

DARNAY. Sir, we have done wrong and are reaping the fruits of wrong.

MARQUIS. We have done wrong?

DARNAY. Our family, whose honour is of so much account to both of us, in such different ways. Even in my father's time, we did a world of wrong, injuring every human creature who came between us and our pleasure. Why need I speak of my father's time when it is equally yours? Can I separate my father's brother, joint inheritor, and next successor, from himself?

MARQUIS. Death has done that.

DARNAY. Yes. And has left me bound to a system that I

am responsible for, but powerless in.

MARQUIS. Better to be a rational creature, and accept your natural destiny. My friend, I will die perpetuating the system under which I have lived. But you are lost, Monsieur Charles, I see.

DARNAY. Your system of governing and this stoney fortress are lost to me. I renounce them.

MARQUIS. Are they both yours to renounce? The government may be, but is this property?

DARNAY. I had no intention, in the words I used, to claim it yet. But whenever it becomes mine, I will abandon it and live elsewhere.

MARQUIS. Forgive my curiosity, but how do you, under your new philosophy, graciously intend to live?

DARNAY. I must do what others of my countrymen must do. Work.

MARQUIS. In England, for example.

DARNAY. Yes. The family name, sir, is safe from me in that country, for I do not use it there.

MARQUIS. Indeed! They say, those boastful English, that it is the refuge of many. You know a compatriot who has found refuge there? A doctor?

DARNAY. Yes.

MARQUIS. With a daughter.

DARNAY. Yes.

MARQUIS. Yes. So commences the new philosophy! *(He rings his table bell. K.E. enters; to K.E.)* Light my nephew to his chamber there. *(K.E. exits U.S.R. followed by DAR-NAY; to himself.)* And burn Monsieur my nephew in his bed!

Scene 2c: *The Gorgon's Head*

The four "stone-faces" — JACQUES I, II and two PEASANTS — slowly leave their statuesque positions and begin to transform the long table into the MARQUIS's bed. They become the four corner posts of the bed, holding a white sheet overhead like a canopy. MARQUIS prepares for bed. WOMAN, JACQUES III, GASPARD, who is dressed in a white night shirt, and DEFARGE appear in shadows around the innyard, as if in the MARQUIS' thoughts.

WOMAN. Monseigneur, hear my petition. My husband died of want. So many die of want. So many more will die of want.

JACQUES III. The man rode under your carriage. He was whiter than the miller, white as a sceptre, tall as a sceptre. *(GASPARD moans softly.)*

MARQUIS. *(referring to GASPARD)* Why does he make that abominable noise?

DEFARGE. Excuse me, Monsieur the Marquis. It was his child!

MARQUIS. It is extraordinary to me that you people cannot take care of yourselves and your children. One or the other of you is forever in the way of my carriage. How do I know what injury you have done my horses?

DEFARGE. *(to GASPARD)* Be brave man. It is better for the poor plaything to die than to live in these times. *(WOMAN, JACQUES III, GASPARD and DEFARGE quietly exit.)*

MARQUIS. I am cool now and may go to bed. *(As lights fade out, the last glimmer of light is cast upon the four stone faces.)*

Q. E. *(She appears dimly lit on the U.S.C. loft.)* The human stone faces of the chateau stared blindly at the night. Dead darkness added its own hush to the hushing dust on all the roads. But in that hushed darkness of the night the Gorgon's head surveyed the building again, and had added the one stone face wanting; the stone face for which it had waited two hundred years. *(A single beam of light illuminates the bed. The four "stone-faced" PEASANTS are gone. The canopy is draped over the MARQUIS with a knife driven through his heart. A letter is stuck to the draped corpse with the knife.)* "Drive him fast to his tomb, this from Jacques." *(Blackout. The sound of screaching owls is heard.)*

Scene 3: *Conversations*

The following scene consists of three separate but simultaneous conversations. They are between DR. MANETTE and DARNAY, LORRY and STRYVER, and CARTON and LUCIE. The three conversations take place D.S.L., D.S.C., and D.S.R. As the scene begins, seated on stage in their respective areas are DR. MANETTE — S.L., MR. LORRY — C.S., LUCIE — S.R.

K. F. *(He stands on U.S.L. balcony.)* Now, from the days when it was always summer in Eden, to these days when it is mostly winter in fallen latitudes, the world of a man has invariably gone one way: the way of the love of a woman. *(K. F. exits. DARNAY enters DR. MANETTE's sitting room D.S.L., which is suggested by two chairs. DR. MANETTE stands.)*

DR. MANETTE. Charles Darnay! *(STRYVER enters U.S.C. into Tellson's Bank, suggested by the banker's desk and stool. LORRY is busily working.)*

STRYVER. *(to LORRY)* Halloa.

DARNAY. *(to DR. MANETTE)* Sir!

DR. MANETTE. *(to DARNAY)* I rejoice to see you. *(LORRY glances up from his work for a moment.)*

LORRY. Ah! Mr. Stryver.

DR. MANETTE. We have been counting on your return these three or four days past. *(He motions for DARNAY to sit down.)*

LORRY. *(He continues to work.)* Can I do something for you, Mr. Stryver?

STRYVER. Why, no, thank you. *(He begins to pace. CARTON enters D.S.R., where LUCIE has been sitting on a bench. She does not see him.)*

DR. MANETTE. Mr. Stryver and Mr. Carton were both here yesterday and made you out to be more than due.

DARNAY. I'm obliged to them for their interest in the matter.

DR. MANETTE. Everyone will be delighted with your return.

CARTON & DARNAY. Miss Manette? *(LUCIE is startled.)*

CARTON. *(to LUCIE)* How are you today?

LUCIE. *(surprised)* Mr. Carton! I'm fine. Thank you.

DR. MANETTE. *(to DARNAY)* Lucie has presently gone

out on some household matters...

DARNAY. I knew she was from home. I took the opportunity to beg to speak to you.

STRYVER. Rather, Mr. Lorry, I come for a private word with you.

LORRY. Oh, indeed.

CARTON. *(to LUCIE)* Pray forgive me. I wish to speak to you. Will you hear me?

LUCIE. Most certainly, Mr. Carton.

DR. MANETTE. Is Lucie the topic?

DARNAY. She is.

STRYVER. *(to LORRY)* I am on my way to offer myself in marriage to your agreeable little friend, Miss Manette. She is a charming creature, and I have made up my mind to please myself.

LORRY. Oh, dear me.

DARNAY. *(to DR. MANETTE)* You anticipate what I would say, though you cannot know how earnestly I say it. Dear Doctor Manette, I love your daughter.

CARTON. *(to LUCIE)* If it had been possible that you could have returned the love of the man you see before you — this creature of misuse that you know him to be...

STRYVER. Well, Mr. Lorry...

CARTON. He would have been conscious, in spite of his happiness, that he would pull you down with him.

LORRY. *(to STRYVER)* Were you going there now?

STRYVER. Straight!

CARTON. *(to LUCIE)* And yet, knowing the misery he would bring you...

LORRY. *(to STRYVER)* I think I wouldn't if I were you.

STRYVER. Well! *(He turns away from LORRY.)*

CARTON. He has still the weakness to wish you to know with what a sudden mastery you kindled him.

DARNAY. *(He gently trys to press on; to DR. MANETTE)* Sir!

DR. MANETTE. I do not doubt your loving Lucie, you may be satisfied of that.

CARTON. Even in my degradation the sight of you with your father, the visits to your home, have stirred old shadows that I thought had died out of me.

DARNAY. Between you and Miss Manette there is an affection so unusual, so much more than even the tenderness between father and child, that I have forborn as long as it was in the nature of man to do so. But I love her.

DR. MANETTE. You speak feelingly, Charles Darnay. I thank you for it.

STRYVER. Damn me! But this beats everything. A man of business deliberately advises me not to go to the Manettes and offer myself — myself, Stryver of the King's Bench Bar.

LORRY. I think in terms of your success with the young lady. I wouldn't go on such an object without having some cause to believe that I should succeed.

DR. MANETTE. Have you any reason to believe that Lucie loves you?

DARNAY. None. As yet, none.

CARTON. I know very well that you can have no tenderness for me. I ask for none. I am even thankful that it cannot be.

LUCIE. Without it, can I not save you, Mr. Carton? Can

I in no way repay your confidence? I know this is a confidence; I know you would say this to no one else.

CARTON. If you will hear me through a very little more, all you can ever do for me is done.

DR. MANETTE. Is it the immediate object of this confidence, that you may at once ascertain Lucie's feelings, with my knowledge?

DARNAY. Not even so.

STRYVER. How then, Mr. Lorry, does one inquire of his success or failure in such matters?

DR. MANETTE. Then you seek a promise from me?

DARNAY. I do seek that.

CARTON. Will you let me believe, when I recall this day, that this confidence will be shared by no one?

LUCIE. The secret is yours, not mine. I promise to respect it.

CARTON. Thank you.

DARNAY. If Miss Manette should bring to you a confidence that she should love me as I love her, I ask you to bear testimony to what I have said and urge no influence against me. I say nothing more of my stake in this.

STRYVER. Mr. Lorry?

LORRY. I was about to say, Mr. Stryver, it might be painful for the Manettes to have the task of being explicit with you. If you please, representing you in no way, I will attempt to correct my advice by making a trip to their home. If my findings should support what I have advised, it may spare all sides what is best spared. What do you say?

STRYVER. I say yes. I am not that hot upon it. I shall expect you to look in tonight. Good morning. *'He exits followed by LORRY.)*

DR. MANETTE. I believe your object to be truthfully as you have stated it. If she should ever tell me that you are essential to her perfect happiness, which is foremost, I will give her to you.

DARNAY. Your confidence in me ought to be returned with full confidence on my part. My present name, though slightly changed from my mother's, is not my own. I wish to tell you what that is, and why I am in England.

DR. MANETTE. Stop.

CARTON. For you, and for anyone dear to you, I would embrace any sacrifice.

DR. MANETTE. Tell me when I ask you!

CARTON. The time will come...

DR. MANETTE. If your suit should prosper...

CARTON. When new ties will be formed about you, ties that will bind you yet more tenderly and strongly to the home you so adorn.

DR. MANETTE. If Lucie should love you...

CARTON. The dearest ties that will ever grace and gladden you.

DR. MANETTE. You shall tell me on the eve of your marriage.

DARNAY. Willingly.

CARTON. When you see your own bright beauty springing up anew at your feet, think now and then that there is a man who would give his life, to keep a life you love beside you.

DR. MANETTE. *(to DARNAY)* Give me your hand. *(CARTON takes LUCIE's hand.)* She will be home directly, and it is better that she not see us together. Go.

CARTON. Farewell.

DR. MANETTE & CARTON. God bless you! *(Lights fade out on DR. MANETTE/DARNAY and CARTON/LUCIE. Everyone exits. STRYVER enters and crosses D.S.C. LORRY enters from U.S.R.)*

LORRY. *(to STRYVER)* I have been to the Manettes.

STRYVER. To the Manettes? Oh to be sure. What am I thinking of?

LORRY. And I have no doubt that I was right in the conversation we had. Therefore, I reiterate my advice.

STRYVER. I assure you that I am sorry for it on your account, and sorry for it on the poor father's account. I know this must always be a sore subject with the family. Let us say no more about it.

LORRY. I don't understand.

STRYVER. Well, no matter.

LORRY. But it does matter.

STRYVER. No it doesn't. I assure you it doesn't. Having supposed that there was sense where there is no sense, I am well out of my mistake, and no harm is done. I have not proposed to the young lady, and, between ourselves, I am by no means certain that I ever should have committed myself to that extent. I am very much obliged to you though for allowing me to sound you out, and for giving me your advice. Now, pray say no more about it. Thank you again. *(LORRY abruptly exits. Slow fade out on STRYVER, who can no longer suppress his emotions.)*

Scene 4a: *Jacques III*

Q.E. enters and stands under the street lamp slung from the guillotine.

Q.E. All France itself lay under the night sky. But then, so does a whole world, with all its greatnesses and littlenesses, lie in a twinkling star. *(DEFARGE and M. DEFARGE enter D.S.R.)*

Madame Defarge. *(to DEFARGE)* Say then, my friend, what did Jacques of the police tell thee?

Defarge. Very little tonight, but all he knows. There is another spy commissioned for our quarter.

Madame Defarge. Eh well! It is necessary to register him. How do they call the man?

Defarge. He is English.

Madame Defarge. So much the better. His name?

Defarge. Barsad.

Madame Defarge. Good. Christian name?

Defarge. John.

Madame Defarge. His age?

Defarge. Forty years.

Madame Defarge. Appearance?

Defarge. Height — six foot; dark hair and mutton chops. *(He sits on D.S.R. step.)*

Madame Defarge. You are fatigued.

Defarge. I am a little tired.

Madame Defarge. You are a little depressed, too. Oh, the men, the men!

DEFARGE. But my dear! It is a long time.

MADAME DEFARGE. When is it not a long time? Vengeance and retribution require a long time. It is the rule.

DEFARGE. It does not take a long time to strike a man with lightning.

MADAME DEFARGE. How long does it take to make and store the lightning? It does not take a long time for an earthquake to swallow a town. Eh well! Tell me how long it takes to prepare the earthquake?

DEFARGE. A long time, I suppose.

MADAME DEFARGE. But when it is ready, it takes place and grinds to pieces everything before it. That is your consolation. Keep it.

DEFARGE. But my brave wife, it has lasted a long time, and it is possible that it may not come during our lives. We shall not see the triumph.

MADAME DEFARGE. We shall have helped it. Nothing we do is done in vain. I believe that we shall see the triumph. But even if I knew certainly not, show me the neck of an aristocrat and still I would...

DEFARGE. Hold! I too, my dear, will stop at nothing.

MADAME DEFARGE. Yes! But it is your weakness that you sometimes need to see your victim and your opportunity to sustain you. Sustain yourself without that. *(Spotting JACQUES III U.S.C., she crosses U.S.L to wine shop. She enters wine shop, has a brief conversation with JACQUES I and II and then sends them out on the street to meet DEFARGE. Meanwhile, JACQUES III crosses S.R. to DEFARGE. JACQUES I and II join them.)*

DEFARGE. Jacques One, Jacques Two! This is the witness. Speak.

JACQUES III. Where shall I commence, monsieur?

DEFARGE. Commence at the commencement.

JACQUES III. I saw him then, messieurs, a year ago this running summer, underneath the carriage of the Marquis.

JACQUES I. Had you ever seen the man before?

JACQUES III. Never.

JACQUES II. How did you afterwards recognize him?

JACQUES III. By his tall figure. When Monsieur the Marquis demands "What is he like?" I make response, tall as a spectre.

JACQUES II. You should have said, short as a dwarf.

JACQUES III. But what did I know? The deed was not then accomplished.

DEFARGE. He is right. Go on.

JACQUES III. The tall man is sought ... How many months? Nine, ten?

DEFARGE. No matter the number. He is well hidden, but at last he is unluckily found. Go on!

JACQUES III. I am again upon the road, when I see coming six soldiers. In the midst of them is a tall man with his arms bound, tied to his sides like this. They drive him with their guns, like this! I follow. As they descend the hill like madmen running a race, he falls. They laugh and pick him up again. His face is bleeding and covered with dust, but he cannot touch it. Thereupon, they laugh again. They bring him into the village, and up to the prison. All the village sees the prison gate swallow him — like this! (*He opens his mouth as wide as he can and shuts it with a sounding snap of his teeth. He is hesitant to mar the effect by opening his mouth again.)*

DEFARGE. Go on, Jacques.

JACQUES III. All the village whispers that, although condemned to death, he will not be executed. They say that petitions showing that he was enraged and made mad by the death of his child have been presented to the King himself. What do I know? It is possible. Perhaps yes, perhaps no.

DEFARGE. Enough! Long live the Devil! Go on.

JACQUES III. Well! Some whisper this, some whisper that. At length, gallows forty feet high are constructed over the fountain. Soldiers march into the prison in the night. He is bound as before, and taken to the fountain and hanged — and left hanging, poisoning the water. It is frightful, messieurs. How can the women and the children draw water? When I left the village at sunset, I looked back from the hill. The shadow struck across the church, seemed to strike across the earth, messieurs, to where the sky rests upon it. That's all, messieurs. I walked on that night and half the next day. And here you see me.

DEFARGE. Good. You have acted and recounted well. Wait for me there.

JACQUES III. Very willingly.

JACQUES I. How say you, Jacques? To be registered?

DEFARGE. To be registered, as doomed to destruction.

JACQUES II. Magnificient.

JACQUES I. The chateau and all the race?

DEFARGE. The chateau and all the race. Extermination.

JACQUES I. Are you sure that no embarrassment can arise from our manner of keeping the register? Without doubt it is safe, for no one beyond ourselves can decipher it; but will she always be able to decipher it?

DEFARGE. Knitted in her own symbols, it will always be as plain to her as the sun. Confide in Madame Defarge.

JACQUES II. *(referring to JACQUES III)* Is this rustic to be sent back soon? Is he not a little dangerous?

DEFARGE. He knows nothing, at least nothing more than would easily elevate himself to the gallows. I charge myself with him. He wishes to see the fine world — The King, the Queen and the court.

JACQUES I. What? Is it a good sign that he wishes to see nobility?

DEFARGE. Show a cat milk, if you wish her to thirst for it. Show a dog his natural prey, if you wish him to bring it down one day. *(JACQUES I and II exit. K. F. and Q. F. appear on U. S. C. loft costumed in royal garb as in the first scene. JACQUES III rejoins DEFARGE. They watch royal pair.)*

JACQUES III. Long live the King, long live the Queen, long live everybody and everything. *(He continues to carry on like a child — whistling, etc.)*

DEFARGE. *(to JACQUES III)* Bravo! You are a good boy! You are the fellow we want. You make these fools believe that it will last forever. Then they are the more insolent, and it is nearer. *(DEFARGE and JACQUES III exit D. S. R.)*

Scene 4b: *The Spy*

VENGEANCE enters from U.S.R. and crosses to wine shop. BAR-SAD enters U.S.R. and follows her inside. MADAME DEFARGE is seated at her knitting.

BARSAD. Good evening, madame.

MADAME DEFARGE. Good evening, monsieur.

BARSAD. Have the goodness to give me a glass of old cognac. You appear to knit with great skill, madame.

MADAME DEFARGE. I am accustomed to it.

BARSAD. A pretty pattern too!

MADAME DEFARGE. You think so?

BARSAD. Decidedly. May one ask what it is for?

MADAME DEFARGE. Pastime.

BARSAD. Not for use?

MADAME DEFARGE. That depends. I may find a use for it one day. If I do ... well, I'll use it.

BARSAD. You have a husband?

MADAME DEFARGE. I have.

BARSAD. Children?

MADAME DEFARGE. No children.

BARSAD. Business seem bad?

MADAME DEFARGE. Business is very bad. The people are so poor.

BARSAD. Ah, the unfortunate, miserable people! So oppressed, too — as you say.

MADAME DEFARGE. As you say.

BARSAD. Pardon me; certainly it was I who said so, but you naturally think so.

MADAME DEFARGE. I think? All we think here is how to live. And it gives us, from morning to night, enough to think about. I think for others? No, no.

BARSAD. A bad business this, of Gaspard's execution. Ah! The poor Gaspard.

MADAME DEFARGE. If people use knives for such purposes, they have to pay for it. He knew beforehand what the price of his luxury was.

BARSAD. I believe there is much compassion and anger in this neighborhood for the poor fellow? Between ourselves...

MADAME DEFARGE. Is there?

BARSAD. Is there not? *(DEFARGE enters wine shop.)* Good day, Jacques! Good day, Jacques.

DEFARGE. You deceive yourself, monsieur, you mistake me for another. I am Ernest Defarge.

BARSAD. It is all the same, good day!

DEFARGE. Good day!

BARSAD. I was saying to madame, that they tell me there is — and no wonder — much sympathy and anger touching the unhappy fate of poor Gaspard.

DEFARGE. No one has told me so.

BARSAD. The pleasure of conversing with you, Monsieur Defarge, recalls an interesting association with your name.

DEFARGE. Indeed!

BARSAD. Yes, indeed. When Doctor Manette was released, you, his old servant, had charge of him.

DEFARGE. Such is the fact, certainly.

BARSAD. It was to you that his daughter came; and it was from your care that his daughter took him over to England.

DEFARGE. Such is the fact.

BARSAD. Very interesting remembrance! I have known Doctor Manette and his daughter in England.

DEFARGE. Yes?

BARSAD. You don't hear much about them now?

DEFARGE. No.

MADAME DEFARGE. In effect, we never hear about them. We received the news of their safe arrival and perhaps another letter. Since then, they have gradually taken their road in life and we ours.

BARSAD. She is going to be married.

MADAME DEFARGE. Going? She was pretty enough to have been married long ago. You English are very cold it seems to me.

BARSAD. But not to an Englishman; to one who, like herself, is French by birth. And speaking of Gaspard — ah, poor Gaspard — it is a curious thing that she is going to marry the nephew of Monsieur the Marquis, for whom Gaspard was exalted to that height of so many feet. In other words, she is to marry the present Marquis. But he lives unknown in England. He is no Marquis there. He is Mr. Charles Darnay. D'Aulnais is the name of his mother's family. Marvelous cognac. I look forward to seeing both of you again soon. *(He exits.)*

DEFARGE. Can it be true?

MADAME DEFARGE. As he has said it, it is probably false. But it may be true.

DEFARGE. If it is...

MADAME DEFARGE. If it is?

DEFARGE. I hope for her sake destiny will keep her husband out of France.

MADAME DEFARGE. *(referring to knitting)* Her husband's destiny, recorded here, will lead him to the end that is to end him. That is all I know.

DEFARGE. But is it not very strange that after all our sympathy for her and her father that her husband's name should be prescribed there next to Barsad's?

MADAME DEFARGE. Stranger things than that will happen when it does come. I have them both here, and they are both here for their merits. That is enough.

Scene 5: *Footsteps*

Cross fade from wine shop to bench positioned D.S.L. The place is Soho Square, London. LUCIE and DR. MANETTE enter and sit on bench.

Q. E. All France itself lay under the night sky. But so does a whole world, with all its greatnesses and littlenesses, lie in a twinkling star.

LUCIE. You are happy, Father?

DR. MANETTE. Quite, my child.

LUCIE. And so am I, Father. But if my marriage would part us, I would be more unhappy than I could tell you. Even as it is, do you feel quite sure that no new affections or duties of mine will ever interpose between us?

DR. MANETTE. Quite sure, my dear! You cannot fully appreciate the anxiety I have felt that your life should not be wasted — for my sake. Thousands of times in my prison cell I thought about the unborn child from whom I had been taken. Whether it had been born alive, or the poor mother's despair had killed it. Whether it was a son who would some day avenge his father, for there was a time in my imprisonment when my desire for vengeance was unbearable. Whether it was a daughter who would grow to be a woman; I imagined her coming to me in my cell and leading me out into the freedom beyond the fortress. Can you follow me, Lucie? Hardly, I think. You must be a solitary prisoner to understand these things. Lucie, I recall these old troubles tonight, because I love you more than words can tell. I am thankful to God for my great happiness. My thoughts, when they were wildest, never rose near the happiness that I have known with you, and that we have before us. (*CHARLES DAR-NAY enters D.S.L. and crosses to them.*)

LUCIE. Charles!

DR. MANETTE. Good evening, Mr. Darnay.

DARNAY. Good evening. Lucie, may I have a word with your father?

LUCIE. Most certainly.

DARNAY. Thank you. (*He kisses her hand. LUCIE exits. To DR. MANETTE.*) Do you remember a previous occasion when I spoke to you of my love for your daughter?

DR. MANETTE. Yes.

DARNAY. At that time, I spoke of my present name and how it was slightly changed from my mother's, but that it was not my own.

DR. MANETTE. Mr. Darnay...

DARNAY. You stopped me then as you stop me now. I wish to keep no secrets from you.

DR. MANETTE. I have watched the two of you together, that is all that I need be concerned with.

DARNAY. But, sir, we had an understanding. If one day I would win Lucie's hand, I could then speak confidentially with you about my heritage. I know that you are troubled by memories of your imprisonment in France; but it is precisely for that reason that I must speak to you. Sir, I was born into the ranks of French nobility, which has done wrong to so many. But I have renounced all association with my father's name and property.

DR. MANETTE. And your father's name, Mr. Darnay?

DARNAY. Evremonde ... Sir?

DR. MANETTE. *(after a moment)* Thank you for sharing this confidence with me. May we go inside now? *(They both exit.)*

Scene 6: *The Wedding*

Q.F. There was no one bidden to the marriage but Mr. Lorry. There was no bridesmaid but Miss Pross. The following morning they all went to the neighboring church where Charles and Lucie were happily married. *(This scene takes place in the parlor of the Manette's, as suggested in Act II, Sc. 1, with two chairs, bench and sideboard.*

MR. LORRY, DR. MANETTE and DARNAY enter. DR. MANETTE sits on bench.) When the newly-married pair arrived home, prior to leaving for the country, Sydney Carton came to offer his congratulations. *(CARTON enters through doorway, greets LORRY and begins to cross to DARNAY. MISS PROSS enters U.S.L. with luggage.)*

LORRY. *(to MISS PROSS)* And so it was for this that I brought my sweet Lucie across the Channel, such a baby! How little I thought of what I was doing! How lightly I valued the obligation I was conferring on my friend, Mr. Charles!

MISS PROSS. You didn't mean it, and therefore how could you know it? Nonsense! Come! *(She and LORRY exit U.S.L. for more luggage.)*

CARTON. Mr. Darnay, I wish we might be friends.

DARNAY. We are already friends, I hope.

CARTON. You remember a certain famous occasion when I was more drunk than usual?

DARNAY. I remember a certain famous occasion when you forced me to confess that you had been drinking.

CARTON. The curse of that occasion is heavy upon me. On that occasion I was insufferable about not liking you. I wish you would forget it.

DARNAY. I forgot it long ago.

CARTON. If you could endure to have such an insufferable fellow around, I should ask that I might be permitted to drop in as a privileged person in your home. I doubt if I should avail myself of it four times a year. It would satisfy me to know that I had it.

DARNAY. Most certainly!

CARTON. I thank you, Darnay. *(PROSS, LORRY and*

LUCIE enter U.S.L CARTON crosses to LUCIE.) My congratulations, Miss Manette.

LUCIE. Thank you, Mr. Carton.

CARTON. *(awkwardly)* Well, then ... have a pleasant trip. *(He exits.)*

DARNAY. Sydney is such a case of carelessness and recklessness.

LUCIE. Charles, Mr. Carton deserves more consideration and respect than you express. Remember how strong we are in our happiness, and how weak he is in his misery.

DARNAY. Lucie, you are my life. *(They kiss. LUCIE sees her father standing behind DARNAY.)*

LUCIE. Father!

DR. MANETTE. Yes, my child. *(They embrace. To DARNAY.)* Take her Charles. She is yours. *(He exits U.S.L followed by MISS PROSS.)*

LORRY. You leave your good father in hands as earnest and as loving as your own. When he joins you at a fortnight's end, you shall say that we have sent him in the best health and in the happiest frame. Let me kiss my dear girl with an old-fashioned bachelor blessing. *(LORRY shakes DARNAY's hand. DARNAY and LUCIE exit U.S.R. through doorway. Lights begin slowly to fade. There is the sudden unexpected sound of the cobbler's hammer, as heard earlier in "The Shoemaker" scene — Act I, Sc. 4c.)* Good God! What is that? *(Lights bump up to full as MISS PROSS enters hurriedly from U.S.L)*

MISS PROSS. All is lost! What is to be told to Ladybird? He doesn't know me and is making shoes! *(Blackout)*

Scene 7: *An Opinion*

DR. MANETTE and MR. LORRY are revealed sitting at a break-fast table C.S. MISS PROSS enters, removes dishes from table, gives MR. LORRY a supportive glance and then exits.

LORRY. My dear Manette, I am anxious to have your opinion in confidence on a case in which I am deeply interested. The case is that of a particularly dear friend of mine. Pray give your mind to it and advise me well for his sake, and above all, for his daughter's.

DR. MANETTE. Be explicit. Spare no detail.

LORRY. It is the case of an old and prolonged shock, of great severity, affecting the mind. It is the case of a shock under which the sufferer was borne down, one cannot say for how long, because I believe he cannot calculate the time himself, and there are no other means of getting at it. It is the case of a shock from which the sufferer recovered so completely, as to be a highly intelligent man. Unfortunately, there has been a slight relapse.

DR. MANETTE. Of how long duration?

LORRY. Nine days and nights.

DR. MANETTE. *(he glances at his leather-stained hands.)* How did it show itself? Was it in the resumption of some old pursuit connected with the shock?

LORRY. That is the case.

DR. MANETTE. Had you ever seen him engaged in that pursuit originally?

LORRY. Once.

DR. MANETTE. And when the relapse fell on him, was he in most respects as he was then?

LORRY. I think in all respects.

DR. MANETTE. You spoke of his daughter. Does his daughter know of the relapse?

LORRY. No. It has been kept from her, and I hope will always be kept from her. It is known only to myself, and to one other who may be trusted.

DR. MANETTE. *(grasping LORRY's hand)* That was very kind.

LORRY. Now, my dear Manette, I am a mere man of business and unfit to cope with such intricate and difficult matters. I want guiding. There is no man on whom I could so rely for right guidance. Pray discuss it with me. Enable me to see it a little more clearly.

DR. MANETTE. I think it probable that the relapse you have described, my dear friend, was not quite unforseen by its subject.

LORRY. Was it dreaded by him?

DR. MANETTE. Very much.

LORRY. Would he be sensibly relieved if he could impart that secret brooding to anyone?

DR. MANETTE. I think so. But that would be next to impossible.

LORRY. Now, to what would you refer this attack?

DR. MANETTE. I believe some intense association with the first cause of this condition was vividly recalled. It is probable that he had long dreaded the return of these associations. He tried to prepare himself; perhaps the effort to prepare himself made him less able to bear it.

LORRY. Would he remember what took place in the relapse?

DR. MANETTE. Not at all.

LORRY. Now, as to the future...

DR. MANETTE. As it pleased Heaven to restore him so soon, I should have great hope for the future. I should hope that the worst was over.

LORRY. I am thankful.

DR. MANETTE. I am thankful.

LORRY. There is one other point on which I am anxious to be instructed. I may go on?

DR. MANETTE. You cannot do your friend a better service.

LORRY. The occupation resumed under the influence of this passing affliction, we will call blacksmith's work. We will say, for the sake of illustration, that in his bad time, he would work at a little forge. We will say that he was unexpectedly found at his forge again. Is it not a pity that he should keep it by him? Would it not be better that he should let it go?

DR. MANETTE. You see it is very hard to explain the inner-most workings of his mind. He once yearned for that occupation, and it was so welcome when it came. No doubt it relieved his pain — substituting the perplexity of the fingers for the perplexity of the brain. Even now, when I believe he is more hopeful of himself than he has ever been, the idea that he might need that old employment, and not find it, gives him such a sudden sense of terror.

LORRY. But may not the retention of the thing involve the retention of the idea? If the thing were gone, my dear

Manette, might not the fear go with it?

DR. MANETTE. You see, too, it is such an old companion.

LORRY. I would not keep it. I would recommend him to sacrifice it. I only want your authority. Come! For his daughter's sake.

DR. MANETTE. In her name then, let it be done. Let it be removed when he is not there; let him miss his old companion after an absence. (*Lights fade out on LORRY and DR. MANETTE.*)

Q. F. They passed the day in the country and the Doctor was quite restored. On the fourteenth day he went away to join Lucie and her husband. That evening, Mr. Lorry went into the Doctor's room with a chopper, saw, chisel, and hammer, attended by Miss Pross. There, with closed doors, and in a mysterious and guilty manner, like accomplices in a horrible crime, Mr. Lorry hacked the shoemaker's bench to pieces. (*Blackout*)

Scene 8a: *Echoing Footsteps*

As the scene begins, the four INNKEEPERS are seated on stairs or stoops in the four corners of the innyard, which should be cleared of all remaining furniture and set pieces. Q.F. holds in her lap a folded tricolor.

K. F. When Charles Darnay and his bride returned to London, they set up housekeeping in the doctor's home located on that street corner full of echoes.

Q. F. Lucie often sat in their parlor listening to the echoing footsteps of the passing years.

K. F. Among the advancing echoes came the tread of tiny feet.

Q. E. But those echoes rarely answered to the actual tread of Sydney Carton. A half-dozen times a year, at most, he claimed his privilege of dropping by.

Q. F. And one other thing regarding him was whispered in the echoes, which has been whispered by all true echoes for ages. No man ever really loved a woman, lost her, and then stopped loving her when she was a wife and a mother.

K. F. Mr. Stryver shouldered his way through the law like some great engine forcing itself through turbid water, and dragged his useful friend, Mr. Carton, in his wake.

K. E. Stryver married a rich widow to whom he often declaimed on the arts Mrs. Darnay had once put in practice to "catch" him, but how he was not to be caught. Some of his King's Bench familiars excused him for this, saying that he had told it so often, that he believed it himself. *(Q. F. moves to the center of the courtyard, where she is met by the other three INNKEEPERS. The immense tricolor that she has been holding in her lap has been folded in such a way that she can pass to each of the INNKEEPERS a corner of the flag, which they assist in stretching out over the ground floor of the courtyard.)*

Q. F. These were among the echoes to which Lucie listened. *(A slow, muffled but steady drumbeat is heard from outside of the innyard. As Q. F. continues, the sound becomes louder as THE VENGEANCE, who is beating the drum, appears in the dark passageway.)* But there were other echoes from a distance that rumbled menacingly in the corner all through this space of time. And it was now, about little Lucie's sixth birthday, that they began to have an awful sound, as of a great storm in France with a dreadful sea rising.

Scene 8b: *The Bastille*

Q.F. lifts her corner of the flag slightly and with a flick of her wrist a small ripple in the fabric crosses the tricolor "sea." The ripple is met by a ripple from the opposite corner held by Q.E. As they continue, their ripples develop into waves, which are soon met by additional waves originating from the corners held by K.E. and K.F. Meanwhile, the drum continues to the beat of the waves. The following phrase is spoken by the PEASANTS — first very softly — as they begin to crawl from the peripheral shadows of the innyard to the area under the billowing flag.

PEASANTS. Deep ditches, double drawbridge, stone walls, eight great towers, cannon, muskets, fire and smoke. Through the fire and through the smoke. *(The chant continues to grow in volume and speed, as the billowing of the flag becomes more dynamic. All PEASANTS crawl under the flag, where they conspire the storming of the Bastille. The INNKEEP-ERS continue to hold their corners of the flag — pocketing air underneath — which shapes the tricolor into an amebic form floating in the air. At this moment, when all activity seems to intensify, Q.E. speaks.)*

Q. E.   The hour is come! *(The flag is billowed high in the air and then stretched taut as it's brought quickly to the ground. This compels the PEASANTS, who are underneath, to scatter to the perimeter of the flag. DEFARGE enters and forces the flag to the ground by walking on the billowing fabric.)*

DEFARGE. *(He shouts.)* Jacques One and Two, separate and put yourselves at the head of as many af these patriots as you can. Keep near to me, Jacques Three. Friends, come then! *(Everyone including the INNKEEPERS form a circle around the flag. They join hands and begin the dance of the revolution — The Farandole.)* Hold! Where is my wife? *(MADAME DEFARGE enters.)*

MADAME DEFARGE.   Eh, well! Here you see me! *(She joins the circle.)*

DEFARGE.   Come, then! Patriots and friends, we are ready! The Bastille! *(All hold hands. The chant begins again to the beat of the drum as they dance around the perimeter of the flag.)*

PEASANTS. Deep ditches, double drawbridge, stone walls, eight great towers, cannon, muskets, fire and smoke. Through the fire and through the smoke. *(As the excitement builds, DEFARGE and MADAME DEFARGE leave the circle and run around on the inside and outside of the circle shouting orders.)*

DEFARGE. *(He is heard over the PEASANT's chant.)* Work, comrades all, work! Work, Jacques One, Jacques Two, Jacques One Thousand, Jacques Two Thousand; in the name of all the Angels and of the Devils — which you prefer — work!

PEASANT. Cannon, muskets, fire and smoke; but still the ditch and still the drawbridge. Deep ditches, single drawbridge, stone walls, eight great towers, cannon muskets, fire and smoke. Through the fire and through the smoke. Cannon, muskets, fire and smoke; at last the walls and eight great towers. Cannon, muskets, fire and smoke; at last the walls, and eight great towers.

DEFARGE. Stop! *(The dancing stops. The drum beat softens. DEFARGE points to K.F.)* You there! Show me the North Tower. Quick! *(K.F. joins DEFARGE in the center of the tricolor, which is still encircled by PEASANTS.)*

K.F. I will, but there is no one there.

DEFARGE. What is the meaning of One Hundred and Five, North Tower? Quick!

K.F. The meaning, Monsieur?

DEFARGE. Does it mean a captive or a place of captivity? Or do you mean that I shall strike you dead!

K.F. Monsieur, it is a cell.

DEFARGE. Show it to me!

K.F. Pass this way then. *(DEFARGE, MADAME DE-FARGE, and K.F. exit U.S.R. The dance starts again softly to the beat of the drum, but it quickly builds to a frenetic level. As it builds, every eighth beat is missed. Each time a beat is not heard on the drum a PEASANT falls from the circle until all have fallen except the three INNKEEPERS, who have participated in the dance. The VENGEANCE's drum beating now expresses the rage. DE-FARGE, MADAME DEFARGE and K.F. re-enter.)*

DEFARGE. *(In his hand, which he holds high in the air, he grasps a piece of paper. He shouts.)* Stop! Enough, Vengeance! *(The drum beating stops. The INNKEEPERS stop dancing. They are exhausted.)* At last it is come! *(The lantern slung from the guillotine doorway and lit early in Act I is lowered by K.F. MADAME DEFARGE extinguishes the flame.)*

MADAME DEFARGE. Eh well! Almost. *(Blackout)*

ACT THREE

Scene 1: *Drawn to the Loadstone Rock*

The scene is Tellson's in London, suggested by LORRY's desk and stool and a table with two chairs. LORRY is seated at his desk. DARNAY is leaning over LORRY's desk. K.F. and K.E. are dressed as Monseigneur. K.E. plays chess with STRYVER at table, while K.F., who has been reading, stops to narrate.

K.F. The August of the year one thousand seven hundred and ninety-two has come, and Monseigneur, as a class of people, was by this time scattered far and wide. After boldly reading the Lord's Prayer backwards for a great number of years, Monseigneur chose to disassociate himself from the phenomenon of his not being appreciated or wanted in France and took to his noble heels. Thus Tellson's in London, in extending great liberality to old customers who had fallen from their high estate, became the gathering place of Monseigneur.

DARNAY. *(to LORRY)* Although you are the youngest man that ever lived, I must still suggest to you...

LORRY. I understand. I am too old.

DARNAY. A long journey, uncertain means of travelling, a disorganized country, a city that may not be safe even for you.

LORRY. My dear Charles, you touch some of the

reasons for my going, not for my staying away. It is safe enough for me. Nobody will care to interfere with this old fellow when there are so many people there much better worth interfering with.

DARNAY. Well, I wish I were going myself.

LORRY. Indeed! You wish you were going yourself? And you a Frenchman born?

DARNAY. My dear Mr. Lorry, it is because I am a Frenchman born that the thought has passed through my mind. One cannot help thinking, having abandoned something to the miserable people, that I might have the power to persuade them for restraint. Only last night, when I was talking to Lucie...

LORRY. When you were talking to Lucie. I wonder you are not ashamed to mention the name of Lucie! Wishing you were going to France!

DARNAY. However, I am not going. It is more to the purpose that you say you are.

LORRY. And I am, in plain reality. The truth is, my dear Charles, you can have no conception of the peril in which the books and papers at the French office are involved. The Lord above knows what would happen to numbers of people if our documents were seized or destroyed. Could I allow such a thing to happen to Tellson's, whose bread I have eaten these sixty years, because I am a little stiff about the joints? Why, I am a boy, sir, to half a dozen old cougers here!

DARNAY. How I admire the gallantry of your youthful spirit.

LORRY. Nonsense. When I have executed this little commission, I shall perhaps accept Tellson's proposal to retire. Time enough then, to think about growing old.

DARNAY. And do you really go tonight?

LORRY. I really go tonight, for the case has become too pressing to admit delay.

DARNAY. You take no one with you?

LORRY. I intend to take Jerry. *(LORRY begins to sort through papers on his desk until he comes to a sealed envelope.)* I should think that I have referred this letter to every Monsieur in London! No one can tell me where this gentleman is to be found. *(He reads the address on the envelope.)* "Very pressing. To Monsieur heretofore the Marquis St. Evremonde, of France. Confided to the cares of Messres. Tellson and Company, Bankers, London, England."

K. F. Nephew, I believe — but in any case degenerate successor — of the polished Marquis who was murdered. Happy to say I never knew him.

K. E. Infected with the new doctrines, set himself in opposition to the last Marquis, abandoned the estate when he inherited it and left it to the ruffian herd. They will recompense him now as he deserves.

STRYVER. Hey? Did he though? *(He crosses to LORRY's desk and takes letter.)* Let us look at his infamous name. Damn the fellow! *(DARNAY takes letter from STRYVER.)*

DARNAY. I know the gentleman.

STRYVER. Do you? Well, I am sorry for it. Sorry that a man who instructs youth knows a fellow that abandoned his worldly goods and property to the vilest scum of the earth.

DARNAY. You may not understand the gentleman.

STRYVER. I understand how to put you in a corner, Mr. Darnay. It is a wonder this fellow is not at the head of the butchery mob. Ah, but no, gentlemen. I know something of human nature, and I tell you that you'll never find a fellow like this trusting himself to the mercies of such precious proteges. No, gentlemen, he'll always show 'em a clean pair of heels. Good day! *(He exits.)*

LORRY. Will you take charge of the letter? You know where to deliver it?

DARNAY. Yes, I do. Good day, Mr. Lorry. *(He exits through guillotine doorway and then leans against the framework. Lights fade on Tellson's interior and up on DARNAY. He rips open the letter.)*

K. E. *(the letter)* "Prison of the Abbaye, Paris, June 21, 1792. Monsieur heretofore the Marquis. After having long been in danger of my life at the hands of the village, I have been seized. The crime for which I am imprisoned, and shall lose my life without your so generous help, is treason, in that I have acted against the people for an emigrant. In vain I tell them I have acted for them and not against according to your commands. In vain I tell them that before the confiscation of emigrant property I slackened all taxes and collected no rent, again at the emigrant's command. The only response is, that I have acted for an emigrant. Now Monsieur, for whom I have been true, where is that emigrant? Your afflicted servant, Gabelle." *(While DARNAY reads letter, LORRY takes the assortment of papers on top of his desk and puts them in desk drawer. He stands and exits through the doorway. He is stopped at the door by DARNAY.)*

DARNAY. I have delivered the letter.

LORRY. So soon?

DARNAY. I would not consent to your being charged

with any written answer, but perhaps you will take a verbal one?

LORRY. That I will, and readily, if it is not dangerous.

DARNAY. Not at all, though it is to a prisoner in the Abbaye.

LORRY. What is his name?

DARNAY. Gabelle.

LORRY. And what is the message to the unfortunate Gabelle?

DARNAY. Simply, "that he has received the letter, and will come."

LORRY. Any time mentioned?

DARNAY. He will start upon his journey tomorrow night.

LORRY. My love to Lucie, and to little Lucie. Take precious care of them till I come back. *(He exits U.S.L. DARNAY returns to LORRY's desk in the dimly lit room. He takes pen and paper and begins to write.)*

K.F. Like the mariner in the old story, the winds and streams had driven him within the influence of the Loadstone Rock. He wrote two fervent letters; one was to Lucie explaining the strong obligation he was under to go to Paris.

K.E. The other was to the Doctor, confiding Lucie and their dear child to his care. Yes, the Loadstone Rock was drawing him, and he would sail on until he struck. For he knew of no rock. And that glorious vision of doing good, which deludes so many good minds, arose before him. For in that illusion he even saw himself with the influence to guide this raging revolution that was running so fearfully wild. *(DARNAY puts letter in an envelope and hurriedly exits.)*

Scene 2: *In Secret*

The courtyard is now empty of all furniture and set pieces except for the desk, which is cleared of all Tellson's Bank related props. As the scene begins, there is a great roar from outside the innyard. The PEASANTS enter with DARNAY from D.S.R. As they manhandle DARNAY, they cross U.S.L. to DEFARGE, who stands behind the desk.

JACQUES I. Down with the emigrant!

JACQUES II.   JACQUES III.
Traitor!   Cursed emigrant!

DARNAY. Emigrant? My friends! Do you not see me here in France of my own will?

JACQUES I.   JACQUES III.
Cursed emigrant!   Cursed aristocrat!

JACQUES II. Condemned traitor!

DARNAY. Friends, you are deceived. I am not a traitor.

DEFARGE. Your age, Evremonde? *(DARNAY turns away from the crowd and faces DEFARGE.)*

DARNAY. Thirty-seven.

DEFARGE. Married, Evremonde?

DARNAY. *(He moves toward DEFARGE.)* Yes.

DEFARGE. Where married?

DARNAY. In England.

DEFARGE. *(softly)* Is it you who married the daughter of Doctor Manette?

DARNAY. Yes!

DEFARGE. My name is Defarge. You have heard of me?

DARNAY. My wife came to your wine shop to reclaim her father. Yes!

DEFARGE. In the name of the sharp female newly born and called La Guillotine, why did you come to France?

DARNAY. I have come here in response to this written appeal of a fellow-countryman. Do you not believe it is the truth?

DEFARGE. A bad truth for you. You are consigned, Evremonde, to the prison of La Force.

DARNAY. Just Heaven! Under what law?

DEFARGE. We have new laws, Evremonde.

DARNAY. I am not to be buried there without any communication with the world outside?

DEFARGE. You will see.

DARNAY. It is of the utmost importance that I communicate to Mr. Lorry of Tellson's Bank that I have been thrown into the prison of La Force. Will you do that for me? It is my right.

DEFARGE. I will do nothing for you. Emigrants have no rights. *(He motions to the crowd to remove DARNAY. PEASANTS exit with DARNAY U.S.R. as lights cross fade.)*

Scene 3: *The Grindstone*

The scene is Tellson's in Paris after nightfall. LORRY enters carrying a ledger. He sits at the desk. The VENGEANCE enters courtyard and sits on D.S.R. step. She softly beats on her drum. After a moment, LORRY stands, crosses to the guillotine doorway and looks through the opening at the frightening activities taking place outside. As he turns toward desk, LUCIE, DR. MANETTE, MISS PROSS and LITTLE LUCIE enter from D.S.L.

LORRY. What is this? Lucie! Manette!

LUCIE. O, my dear friend!

LORRY. What has happened? What has brought you here?

LUCIE. My husband!

LORRY. What of Charles?

LUCIE. Here.

LORRY. Here in Paris?

DR. MANETTE. An errand of generosity brought him here unknown to us. He was stopped at the barrier and sent to prison. *(He hears the noise from outside and crosses to guillotine doorway.)* What is that noise?

LORRY. Don't look! Don't look out! The back courtyard. The place is national property now and used as a kind of armory.

DR. MANETTE. My dear friend, I have a charmed life in this city. I have been a Bastille prisoner. There is no patriot in Paris, in France, who would touch me, except to overwhelm me with embraces. My old pain has gained us news of Charles and brought us here. I knew it would be so. It all tended to a good end, my friend. As my beloved child was helpful in restoring me to myself, I will be helpful in restoring the dearest part of herself to her. *(He stands at doorway looking out.)*

LORRY. I had no suspicion even of his being in this fatal place. What prison is he in?

DR. MANETTE. La Force!

LORRY. La Force! If you really have the power you think you have, make yourself known to those devils, and be taken there at once. *(DR. MANETTE crosses through guillotine doorway and exits. Drumbeat softens until it stops altogether. LORRY turns his back to doorway and crosses to LUCIE.)* Courage, my dear Lucie. So far all goes well, much better than it has of late gone with many poor souls. *(DEFARGE and MADAME DEFARGE meet VEN-GEANCE in the courtyard and cross to guillotine doorway. DEFARGE knocks on framework. MADAME DEFARGE stands U.S. of DEFARGE. LORRY crosses to doorway. To DEFARGE.)* Your servant. Do you know me?

DEFARGE. Do you know me?

LORRY. I have seen you somewhere.

DEFARGE. Perhaps at my wine shop. *(MADAME DE-FARGE steps from behind DEFARGE.)*

LORRY. Madame Defarge, surely.

DEFARGE. Yes. She wishes to see the faces of those just arrived so she may recognize the persons. It is for their safety. *(LUCIE crosses to the door.)*

LORRY. My dear, there are frequent risings in the streets here. Although it is not likely they will ever trouble you, Madame Defarge wishes to see those whom she has the power to protect. I state the case, Citizen Defarge? *(DEFARGE nods his head affirmatively. MISS PROSS brings LITTLE LUCIE to the doorway. LITTLE LUCIE touches MADAME DEFARGE's knitting.)*

Madame Defarge. Is this his child? *(LUCIE touches MADAME DEFARGE's knitting hand.)*

Lucie. You know of my husband? *(MADAME DE-FARGE drops her hand.)*

Madame Defarge. Monsieur Charles is alive, that is all. *(to DEFARGE)* It is enough. I have seen them.

Lucie. As a wife and a mother, I implore you to exercise the power you possess in my innocent husband's behalf.

Madame Defarge. The wives and mothers we have seen since we were as little as this child have not been greatly considered. We have known *their* husbands and fathers laid in prison and kept from them often enough. All our lives we have seen women suffer. Is it likely that the trouble of one wife and mother would be much to us now? *(Blackout)*

Scene 4: *The Guillotine*

Lights bump up immediately. The INNKEEPERS are standing around the guillotine doorway in the same positions occupied by the four principle players in the previous scene. They perform the following interlude with quick and easy movements.

Q. F. *(caressing the guillotine)* It was the best cure for headaches.

K. F. It infallibly prevented the hair from turning gray.

Q. F. It imparted a peculiar delicacy to the complexion.

K. F. It was the National Razor which shaved close. It was that sharp female called La Guillotine.

K. E. It was the sign of the regeneration of the human race.

K. F. Models of it were worn on breasts from which the cross was discarded.

Q. F. And it was bowed down to and believed in where the cross was denied. *(Q. F and Q. E. kneel in front of the guillotine and across from each other so that their knees are touching. K. E. kneels on all fours with his head resting on Q. F. & Q. E.'s knees.)*

Q. E. But he who kissed La Guillotine looked through the little window and sneezed into the sack. *(Q. F. and Q. E., with assistance by K. F., flip K. E. over their knees and through the guillotine opening.)*

K. E. It sheared off heads so many, that it and the ground it most polluted were a rotten red. It hushed the eloquent, struck down the powerful, abolished the beautiful and good. *(LUCIE enters D. S. L and sits on a bench.)*

Q. E. Lucie was never sure from hour to hour that the guillotine would not strike off her husband's next day. *(DR. MANETTE appears S. R. and crosses to LUCIE.)*

K. F. Yet among these terrors, the Doctor remained confident that he would save Lucie's husband at last or at least get him brought to trial.

Q.F. For the current of the time swept by so strong and deep and carried the tide away so fiercely, that Charles had already lain in prison one year and three months when the Doctor was thus steady and confident.

Dr. Manette. *(He sits next to LUCIE on the bench.)* Give me your arm, my love. Charles has been summoned.

Lucie. Oh, Father!

Dr. Manette. He has not received the notice yet, but I know that he will. Nothing connected with Charles has been concealed from me. I have had the strongest assurances that I shall save him. *(MADAME DEFARGE enters D.S.R.)* I salute you, citizeness.

Madame Defarge. I salute you, citizen. *(She remains standing D.S.R.)*

Dr. Manette. You are not afraid.

Lucie. I trust in you.

Dr. Manette. Do so implicitly. I have great influence there. The judges are all very friendly to me. Your suspense is nearly ended, my darling; he shall be restored to you within a few hours.

Scene 5a: *Paris Tribunal*

PEASANTS position a table and chair U.S.L for JACQUES I, who will preside over the Tribunal. DR. MANETTE and LUCIE remain seated on the bench D.S.L LORRY, MISS PROSS and

JERRY join them. MADAME DEFARGE remains standing D.S.R. The large tricolor from the Revolution is hung in such a manner as to cover the U.S.C. second storey loft and the area directly below it. The PEASANTS assist with these preparations and then they sit on the stairs and balconies of the innyard. DEFARGE and THE VENGEANCE enter D.S.R. and stand on stairs near MADAME DEFARGE. JACQUES I rings the Tribunal bell to bring order to the hearing. DARNAY is brought into the courtyard by JACQUES II and III. He stands U.S.R. in guillotine doorway.

JACQUES I. Charles Evremonde, called Darnay, is suspected and denounced as an enemy of the Republic. Is the accused openly denounced or secretly?

JACQUES II. Openly.

JACQUES I. By whom?

JACQUES II. Three voices: Ernest Defarge, wine-vendor of Paris.

JACQUES I. Good.

JACQUES II. Therese Defarge, his wife.

JACQUES I. Good.

JACQUES II. Alexandre Manette, physician. *(DR. MANETTE stands in protest.)*

DR. MANETTE. President, I indignantly protest! You know the accused to be the husband of my daughter! Those dear to her are far dearer to me than my life! Who is the false conspirator who says this?

JACQUES I. Citizen Manette, be silent. As to what is dearer to you than life, nothing can be so dear to a good citizen as the Republic. *(PEASANTS roar with approval.)* Listen to what is to follow. Citizen Ernest Defarge, you did good service at the taking of the Bastille?

DEFARGE. I believe so.

VENGEANCE. He was one of the best patriots there! Why not say so? He was among the first to enter the accursed fortress when it fell! *(JACQUES I rings the Tribunal bell.)* I defy that bell! Patriots, I speak the truth!

JACQUES I. Inform the Tribunal of what you did that day within the Bastille.

DEFARGE. I knew that this prisoner, of whom I speak, had been confined in a cell known as One Hundred and Five, North Tower. I knew it from himself. He knew himself by no other name than that, when he made shoes under my care. I resolve when the place shall fall to examine that cell. I did so. In a hole in the chimney I find this written paper. I confide it to the hands of the president. *(He crosses U.S.L. and gives the letter to JACQUES I, who begins to read the letter aloud as the lights slowly fade on the innyard and intensify on the area directly in front of the tricolor, which has been hung U.S.C.)*

JACQUES I. *(from the letter)* "I, Alexandre Manette, unfortunate physician, write this paper in my cell in the Bastille, during the last month of the tenth year of my captivity, 1767. I write it at stolen intervals, under every difficulty. I design to secrete it in the wall of the chimney. Hope has quite departed. I know from terrible warnings I have noted in myself that my reason will not long remain unimpaired, but I solemnly declare that I am at this time in the possession of my right mind and that I write the truth in these my last recorded words. One evening, in December in the year 1757, I was walking on a retired part of the quay by the Seine when a carriage came along behind me, driven very fast. As I stood aside to let that carriage pass, it stopped and a voice called to me... *(K.F. appears in front of tricolor dressed as a French nobleman.)*

K.F. You are Doctor Manette?

Dr. Manette. *(He has remained standing D.S.L in a state of disbelief.)* I am.

K.F. Will you please accompany me?

Dr. Manette. I usually inquire who seeks my assistance, and what is the nature of the case. *(JACQUES I reads from letter.)*

Jacques I. "Another gentleman alighted from the coach." *(MARQUIS ST. EVREMONDE enters U.S.L from behind the tricolor.)*

Marquis. Doctor, your clients are people of condition. As to the nature of the case, we are counting on you to ascertain that for us. Enough. Will you please to come along?

Dr. Manette. *(He addresses all of those present in the innyard.)* I could do nothing but comply. *(He crosses U.S.C. toward the MARQUIS.)*

Jacques I. *(from the letter)* "I describe everything exactly as it took place. The carriage left the streets behind and emerged upon the country road. It presently stopped at a solitary barn. From the time of our alighting at the outer gate, I had heard cries proceeding from inside. The cries grew louder as we made our way inside." *(The tricolor is lowered to the ground revealing the second storey loft and Q.F. lying on a makeshift bed in the inner below.)* "I found the patient, a woman of great beauty, lying on a makeshift bed."

Q. F. My husband, my father, my brother!

DR. MANETTE. *(to Q. F.)* Hush. *(to MARQUIS)* How long has this lasted?

MARQUIS. Since about this hour last night.

DR. MANETTE. She has a husband, a father, and a brother?

MARQUIS. A brother.

DR. MANETTE. I do not address her brother?

MARQUIS. No!

DR. MANETTE. You see, Gentlemen. If I had known what I was coming to see, I could have come provided.

K. F. There is a case of medicine there. *(DR. MANETTE opens medicines and smells them.)* Do you doubt them?

MARQUIS. There is another patient.

DR. MANETTE. Is it a pressing case?

MARQUIS. You had better see. *(DR. MANETTE follows MARQUIS. They ascend the U.S.L. staircase to the second storey loft. As they reach the top landing, lights reveal K. E. lying in a bed of straw.)*

JACQUES I. "My memory remains unshaken. I try it with these details, and I see them all, in this my cell in the Bastille, as I saw them that night. This patient was a young man. Like the girl, he was a commoner. I could see that he was dying of a sword thrust received from twenty to twenty-four hours before."

DR. MANETTE. *(He kneels next to K. E.)* I am a doctor, my poor fellow. Let me examine it.

K. E. I do not want it examined. Let it be.

DR. MANETTE. *(to MARQUIS)* How has this been done, monsieur?

MARQUIS. The crazed young common dog! A serf! He forced my brother to draw upon him.

K.E. Doctor, they are very proud, these nobles, but we common dogs are proud, too. She — have you seen her, Doctor?

DR. MANETTE. I have seen her.

K.E. She is my sister, Doctor. These nobles have had their shameful rights in the virtue of our sisters for many years. She was betrothed to a good young man, too; a tenant of his. We are all tenants of his. The other is his brother. My sister was married many weeks when the brother first saw her and asked that man to lend her to him. He was willing enough. But how did they persuade her husband? You know, Doctor, that it is among the rights of these nobles to harness us common dogs to carts and drive us. Did you also know that it is among their rights to keep us on their grounds all night quieting the frogs, in order that their noble sleep may not be disturbed. They kept my sister's husband out in the mists at night and ordered him back into his harness in the day. It was not long until they persuaded him right out of this world and into the next. Then with that man's kind permission, the brother took my sister away with him. I took my younger sister, for I have another, to a place beyond the reach of this man. She will never be his vassal. Then with a sword, I tracked the brother here. Marquis St. Evremonde, in the days when all these things are to be answered for, I summon you and yours to answer for them. *(K.E. dies. DR. MANETTE and MARQUIS descend stairs to inner-below. DR. MANETTE crosses to Q.F.'s bedside and continues to care for her.)*

Jacques I. "When I returned to the bedside of the young woman, I found her in a state of lethargy, lying like the dead. It was then that I knew her condition to be that of one in whom the first expectations of being a mother have arisen; and it was then that I lost the little hope I had had for her."

Marquis. Is she dead?

Dr. Manette. Not dead, but like to die.

Marquis. What strength there is in these common bodies.

Dr. Manette. There is prodigious strength in sorrow and despair.

Marquis. Doctor, I recommended that your aid should be invited. Your reputation is high, and, as a young man with your fortune to make, you must be mindful of your interests. The things that you see here are things to be seen and not spoken of.

Dr. Manette. Monsieur, in my profession the communications of patients are always received in confidence.

Jacques I. *(from the letter)* "I write with much difficulty. The cold is severe. I am fearful of being detected and consigned to an underground cell and total darkness; hence, I must abridge this narrative. She lingered for a week. I had no opportunity of asking her any questions until I had told the brothers she was faltering. When it came to that, they seemed careless what communications I might hold with her, as if — the thought passed through my mind — I was dying too." *(DR. MANETTE pulls sheet over Q.F.'s face.)*

Marquis. At last she is dead?

DR. MANETTE. She is dead.

MARQUIS. *(to K.F.)* I congratulate you, my brother. *(MARQUIS offers DR. MANETTE a small pouch containing money.)*

DR. MANETTE. Pray excuse me. Under the circumstances, no. *(MARQUIS exits. DR. MANETTE tries to return to LUCIE in the courtroom but K.F. leads him to a table and chair U.S.R. There is pen and paper on the table.)*

JACQUES I. "Early the next morning, I was returned to my home. From the first, I had anxiously considered what I ought to do. I decided to write privately to the Minister, stating the nature of those two cases. I knew what court influence was. I expected that the matter would never be heard of; but I wished to relieve my own mind. I had kept the matter a profound secret, even from my own wife; and this, too, I resolved to state in my letter. I had no apprehension whatever of my real danger. It was the last day of the year. The letter was lying before me just completed when a woman, who was a stranger to me, payed me a visit." *(Q.E. enters U.S.L holding a baby in her arms. She is well dressed. She crosses S.R. to DR. MANETTE.)*

Q.E. My husband is the brother of the Marquis St. Evremonde. I have discovered the main facts of the cruel story involving him and the unfortunate young lady. I have reasons for believing there was a young sister living, and my greatest desire is to help that girl.

DR. MANETTE. I can tell you only that there was such a sister. *(The lighting subtly highlights the prisoner, DARNAY, standing behind them in the guillotine framework.)*

Q.E. *(speaking to baby in her arms)* For his sake, Doctor, I would do all I can to make what poor amends I can. I fear he will never prosper in his inheritance otherwise. If no atonement is made for this now, it will one day be required of him. *(As Q.E. exits, DR. MANETTE begins to cross to inner-below. But tricolor is pulled back up by PEASANTS, thereby covering the inner-below and second storey loft. DR. MANETTE stands in front of tricolor.)*

JACQUES I. 'I sealed my letter and, not trusting it out of my own hands, delivered it myself that day. That evening a man rang at my gate..." *(JACQUES I begins reading the following speech but his voice fades out as DR. MANETTE begins to speak the words.)*

JACQUES I & DR. MANETTE. "An urgent case in the Rue St. Honore, it would not detain me. He had a coach waiting. It brought me here to the Bastille. It brought me to my living grave. I, Alexandre Manette, do this last night of the year 1767, in my unbelievable agony, denounce to the times when all these things shall be answered for. I denounce the Marquis and his whole race to Heaven and to Earth." *(The crowd in the innyard is in an uproar. JACQUES I rings the bell for order. MADAME DEFARGE climbs the D.S.R. stairs to the first landing.)*

MADAME DEFARGE. *(shouting above the noise)* That peasant family so injured was my family! That sister of the mortally wounded boy was my sister! That brother was my brother! Those dead are my dead! Save him now, my Doctor! Save him now!

Scene 5b: *Solomon*

All begin to leave innyard, taking with them the Tribunal furniture pieces. LORRY assists DR. MANETTE as they exit U.S.L. LUCIE, followed by MISS PROSS, cross U.S.R. to DARNAY.

LUCIE. *(to JACQUES I, II and others guarding DARNAY)* If I might touch him! If I might embrace him once! O, good citizens, if you would have so much compassion for us! *(When the guard in command turns toward LUCIE, he is face to face with MISS PROSS. The guard is BARSAD. MISS PROSS screams. LUCIE runs to DARNAY and embraces him. BARSAD attempts to quiet MISS PROSS, while he gestures to JACQUES II and III. They exit with DARNAY followed by LUCIE.)*

MISS PROSS. Oh, Solomon, dear Brother! After not setting eyes upon you or hearing of you for so long a time, do I find you here!

BARSAD. Don't call me Solomon. Do you want to be the death of me?

MISS PROSS. Brother, have I ever been so hard with you that you ask me such a cruel question? *(JERRY CRUNCHER has crossed to MISS PROSS and stands gazing at BARSAD.)*

BARSAD. Then hold your meddlesome tongue. Who's this man?

MISS PROSS. Mr. Cruncher.

BARSAD. Does he think me a ghost?

MISS PROSS. How dreadfully unkind for a brother to give me such a greeting. *(BARSAD kisses MISS PROSS.)*

BARSAD. There. Confound it! I am not surprised to find you here. I knew you were here. I know of most people who are here. I am an official.

MISS PROSS. My English brother Solomon.

CRUNCHER. I say! Might I ask the favor as to whether your name is John Solomon, or Solomon John? And regarding that name of Pross, likewise. That warn't your name over the water.

BARSAD. What do you mean?

CRUNCHER. Well, I don't know all I mean, for I can't call to mind ... But you was a spy, a witness at the Bailey. What in the name of the father of lies was you called at that time? *(CARTON enters from U.S.L.)*

CARTON. Barsad. Don't be alarmed, my dear Miss Pross. I arrived at Mr. Lorry's, to his surprise, yesterday evening. We agreed that I would not present myself until after the trial. I present myself here, to beg a little talk with your brother. I wish for your sake Mr. Barsad was not a sheep of the prison. You see, since last evening, when I first arrived in Paris, I have done some checking on a number of things. And what began as a random thought, an oddity, after seeing this man come from the prison of the Conciergerie, has shaped itself into a purpose, Mr. Barsad.

BARSAD. What purpose? *(LORRY re-enters D.S.L.)*

LORRY. Miss Pross, will you be coming along to the carriage?

CARTON. Ah, Mr. Lorry. Miss Pross's brother, sir, Mr. Barsad.

LORRY. Barsad? Barsad? I have an association with the name and the face.

CARTON. Witness at the Old Bailey trial.

LORRY. Ah, yes, of course. The situation looks grim, does it not, Mr. Carton?

CARTON. Yes, it does. In short, this is a desperate time, when desperate games must be played for desperate stakes. Now, the stake I have resolved to play for is a friend in the Conciergerie. And the friend I propose to win is Mr. Barsad.

BARSAD. You need have good cards, sir.

CARTON. I'll run them over for you. You'll see what cards I hold. Pray sit down. Jerry, perhaps you might escort Miss Pross, the Doctor, and his daughter home. *(to LORRY)* I wish that you might hear this. *(JERRY and MISS PROSS exit D.S.L)* Now, Mr. Barsad represents himself to his employers under a false name. That's a very good card. Mr. Barsad, now in the employ of the Republican French government, was formerly in the employ of the aristocratic English government, the enemy of France and freedom. That's an excellent card. And Mr. Barsad, under the overthrown French government, spied upon Defarge's wine shop. In fact, it is not unlikely that his real name appears in Madame's knitted register. That is a card not to be beaten. Have you followed my hand, Mr. Barsad?

BARSAD. Not to understand your play.

CARTON. I play my ace — denunciation of Mr. Barsad to the nearest Section Committee. Look over your hand, Mr. Barsad, and see what you have. Don't hurry.

BARSAD. I should have hoped that your respect for my sister...

CARTON. I could not better testify my respect for your

sister than by finally relieving her of her brother. You scarcely seem to like your hand. Do you play?

BARSAD. I must return to the prison. You told me you had a proposal. It is of no use asking too much of me. Ask me to put my head in great danger, and I had better trust my life to chances of a refusal than the chances of consent. We are all desperate here. Remember! What do you want with me?

CARTON. You are a turnkey at the Conciergerie.

BARSAD. I tell you there is no such thing as an escape possible.

CARTON. Why need you tell me what I have not asked? You can pass in and out when you choose? Would you ensure me access to Mr. Darnay — just once?

BARSAD. That is what you ask? ... Agreed.

CARTON. At two tomorrow. Adieu then, Mr. Barsad. (*BARSAD exits.*)

LORRY. But access to him will not save him.

CARTON. I never said it would. You are a good man and a true friend. Yours is a long life to look back upon.

LORRY. I am in my seventy-eighth year.

CARTON. See what a place you fill at seventy-eight. How many people will miss you when you leave it empty?

LORRY. A solitary old bachelor. There is nobody to weep for me.

CARTON. How can you say that? Wouldn't she weep for you? Wouldn't her child?

LORRY. Yes, yes, thank God. I didn't quite mean what I said.

CARTON. It is a thing to thank God for, is it not? If you could truthfully say to your own solitary heart tonight, "I have secured for myself the love and attachment, the gratitude and respect of no human creature; I have done nothing good or serviceable to be remembered by;" your seventy-eight years would be seventy-eight heavy curses, would they not?

LORRY. You say truly, Mr. Carton. I think they would be.

CARTON. But on with my purpose. Your duties here have drawn to an end?

LORRY. Yes. As I was telling you last night, I have at length done all that I can do here at the bank. I have my leave to pass. (*CARTON takes out his certificate for passage.*)

CARTON. This is the certificate which enables me to pass out of this city. Keep it with yours until tomorrow. I shall see him tomorrow, and I had better not take it into the prison.

LORRY. Why not?

CARTON. I prefer not to do so. Now, Dr. Manette, Lucie and her daughter also have such certificates. But they may be soon recalled, and I have reason to think, will be.

LORRY. They are not in danger?

CARTON. They are in great danger. You know it is a capital crime to mourn for a victim of the guillotine. You follow me? Don't look so horrified. You will save tham all.

LORRY. Heaven grant that I may.

CARTON. Early tomorrow have your horses ready at

two o'clock in the afternoon. Tell her tonight what you know of her danger as involving her child and her father. Dwell upon that for she would lay her own fair head beside her husband's. Quietly and steadily have all these arrangements made in the courtyard, even to the taking of your own seat in the carriage. The moment I come to you, take me in, and then for England.

LORRY. I understand that I wait for you under all circumstances?

CARTON. You have my certificate, do you not? Promise me solemnly that nothing will influence you to alter the course on which we now stand pledged to one another.

LORRY. Nothing, Carton.

CARTON. Remember. If you change the course or delay it for any reason, many lives will be sacrificed.

LORRY. I will remember. I hope to do my part faithfully.

CARTON. And I hope to do mine. Good-bye. *(They both exit.)*

Scene 6: *The Shadow*

MADAME DEFARGE, VENGEANCE and JACQUES III appear on D.S.R. staircase.

JACQUES III. But our Defarge is undoubtedly a good Republican?

VENGEANCE. There is no better in France.

MADAME DEFARGE. Peace, little Vengeance. My husband is a good Republican and a bold man. But my husband has his weaknesses, and he is so weak as to relent towards this Doctor. I care nothing for this Doctor. He may wear his head or lose it, for any interest I have in him. But the Evremonde people are to be exterminated. The wife and child must follow the husband.

JACQUES III. The child also! We seldom have a child there. It is a pretty sight.

MADAME DEFARGE. In a word, I fear that if I delay, there is danger of my husband giving warning, and then they might escape.

JACQUES III. That must never be. No one must escape. We have not half enough as it is. We ought to have six score a day.

MADAME DEFARGE. She will now be at home, awaiting the moment of his death. She will be mourning. She will be in a state of mind to impeach the justice of the Republic. I will go to her. *(to VENGEANCE)* Take you my knitting and have it ready for me in my usual seat by La Guillotine. I shall be there before the commencement.

Scene 7: *Fifty-Two*

The innyard becomes DARNAY's prison cell. An amber light from a barred window overhead projects a pattern in the dimly lit court-

*yard. A table, a chair and a cot are the set pieces. As the scene
begins, DARNAY is pacing.*

DARNAY. He made shoes. *(BARSAD and CARTON enter
U.S.R. near guillotine doorway/cell door.)*

BARSAD. He has never seen me here. Go you in alone. I
will wait near by. Lose no time! *(CARTON enters cell.)*

CARTON. Of all the people upon earth, you least expected to see me?

DARNAY. I can not believe it to be you. You are not
... a prisoner?

CARTON. No. I am accidentally possessed of a power
over one of the keepers here. I bring you a request from
your wife. You have no time to ask me why I bring it, or
what it means. I have no time to tell you. You must comply. Take off your boots and draw on these of mine.

DARNAY. Carton, there is no escaping from this place.
You will only die with me. It is madness.

CARTON. It would be madness if I asked you to escape;
but do I? Change that cravat for this of mine, your coat
for mine. While you do it, let me take this ribbon from
your hair and shake out your hair like mine! Here are
pen, ink, paper. Write what I dictate. Quick, friend,
quick! Write as I speak. *(DARNAY sits at the table.)*

DARNAY. To whom do I address it?

CARTON. To no one.

DARNAY. Do I date it?

CARTON. No. *(He dictates the following.)* The words that
passed between us long ago, you will readily com-
prehend when you see this. You do remember them, I
know. It is not in your nature to forget. *(to DARNAY)*

Have you written "to forget"?

DARNAY. I have. Is that a weapon in your hand?

CARTON. No, I am not armed.

DARNAY. What is it then?

CARTON. You shall know directly. "I am thankful that the time has come when I can prove my words. That I do so is no subject for regret or grief." *(CARTON holds a vial in his hand. He dabs some of its contents onto a cloth.)*

DARNAY. What vapour is that?

CARTON. Vapour?

DARNAY. Something that crossed me? *(He springs to his feet. CARTON's hand is close by and firmly holds cloth to DARNAY's nose. DARNAY collapses on the floor.)*

CARTON. *(to BARSAD)* Enter there! Come in! *(BARSAD enters through doorway.)* You see? Is your hazard very great?

BARSAD. Not if you are true to the whole of your bargain.

CARTON. I will be true to the death. Now get assistance and take me to the coach.

BARSAD. You?

CARTON. Him, man, with whom I have exchanged. Go out at the gate by which you brought me in. Say I was weak and faint when you brought me out. The parting interview with the prisoner has overpowered me. Take him yourself to the courtyard, place him in the carriage, show him to Mr. Lorry, then tell him to keep his promise and head as fast as he can for England.

BARSAD. Guard! *(JACQUES II enters.)*

JACQUES II. *(referring to DARNAY)* How, then?

BARSAD. The parting interview left him weak and faint.

Lift him and come away! *(BARSAD and JACQUES II exit with DARNAY. Blackout)*

Scene 8: *The Knitting Done*

The following scene is at the temporary Paris lodging of DR. MANETTE and LUCIE. However, all have left except for MISS PROSS and JERRY, who are taking care of the last of the luggage. A few bags are positioned near the U.S.L. staircase.

MISS PROSS. Mr. Cruncher, what do you think of our not starting from this house? Another carriage having already gone from here today, it might awaken suspicion.

JERRY. My opinion, Miss, is as you're right.

MISS PROSS. I am so distracted with fear and hope for our precious creatures. If you were to go before and stop the vehicle and horses from coming here, and were to wait somewhere for me ... The cathedral door. Would it be much out of the way to take me in there?

JERRY. No, Miss.

MISS PROSS. Then go to the posting house straight and make the change.

JERRY. I am doubtful about leaving you, Miss.

MISS PROSS. Think not of me, but of the lives that may depend on both of us. *(JERRY exits with baggage. MISS PROSS exits by way of U.S.L. staircase. After a moment, she returns as MADAME DEFARGE enters S.R.)*

MADAME DEFARGE. The wife of Evremonde; where is she? It will do her no good to keep herself concealed from me at this moment. Good patriots will know what that means.

MISS PROSS. I know your intentions are evil.

MADAME DEFARGE. I demand to see her. Either tell her so or stand out of the way of those stairs and let me go to her! Citizen Doctor! Wife of Evremonde! Child of Evremonde! Any person but this miserable fool, answer the Citizeness Defarge! *(There is silence.)*

MISS PROSS. As long as you don't know whether they are up there or not, you are uncertain what to do. I don't care an English twopence for myself. I know that the longer I keep you here, the greater hope there is for my Ladybird.

MADAME DEFARGE. I will tear you to pieces, but I will have you out of my way.

MISS PROSS. I'll not leave a handful of that dark hair upon your head, if you lay a finger on me! *(MADAME DEFARGE and MISS PROSS begin to fight.)* I am stronger than you. I'll hold you till one or the other of us faints or dies! *(MADAME DEFARGE reaches for a gun in her bosom. MISS PROSS grabs it. There is a struggle. A gun shot is heard. Blackout. After a moment...)*

MISS PROSS'S VOICE. Mr. Cruncher? ... Jerry?

JERRY. Behind you. *(Lights reveal MISS PROSS standing center stage and JERRY standing a few feet up stage of her.)*

MISS PROSS. Jerry? ... Jerry?

JERRY. Over here. *(He reaches for her from behind and takes her by the arm.)* Here I am!

MISS PROSS. Is there any noise in the streets?

JERRY. The usual noises.

MISS PROSS. I don't hear you. What do you say?

JERRY. Gone deaf in an hour? So I'll nod my head.

MISS PROSS. Is there any noise in the streets now?

JERRY. If you don't hear the roll of those dreadful carts, Miss, then it's my opinion that you won't never hear anything in this world ever again.

Scene 9: *Footsteps Die Out Forever*

The cart, which has been returned to its original appearance as a tumbril, is wheeled into the innyard from U.S.L. CARTON is standing in it. The entire cast appears in the innyard.

K. F. And indeed she never did. Along the Paris streets the tumbril carries the day's wine to La Guillotine. If only these tumbrils could change back to what they were — to the carriages of absolute monarchs and feudal nobles, to the wine carts of peasants, back to the Dover Mail. But no. Changeless and hopeless the tumbrils roll along to their journey's end. *(CARTON steps down from the cart and crosses U.S.R. toward guillotine framework.)*

VENGEANCE. Who has seen her? Terese Defarge!

K. F. The murmuring of voices.

VENGEANCE. She has never missed before!

K. F. The upturning of faces.

VENGEANCE. Evremonde will be dispatched in a wink.

K. F. The pressing on of footsteps.

VENGEANCE. Terese, it is the Vengeance calling. *(CAR-TON stands in the center of the guillotine frame.)*

K. F. Like one great heave of water, all flashes away. *(General lighting fades out as red light illuminates guillotine opening. CARTON and guillotine frame are silhouetted with the red light.)*

Q. F. They said of him about the city that night that it was the peacefullest man's face ever beheld there. Many said he looked almost prophetic.

Q. E. I see Barsad, Defarge, The Vengeance, all of the new oppressors perishing after me by this instrument of correction. I see the lives for which I lay down my life, peaceful, prosperous and happy, in that England which I shall see no more.

K. E. I see Lucie with a child upon her bosom, perhaps he bears my name, a man winning his way up in that part of life which once was mine.

CARTON. It is a far, far better thing that I do, than I have ever done. It is a far, far better rest that I go to than I heve ever known. *(Blackout)*

—THE END—

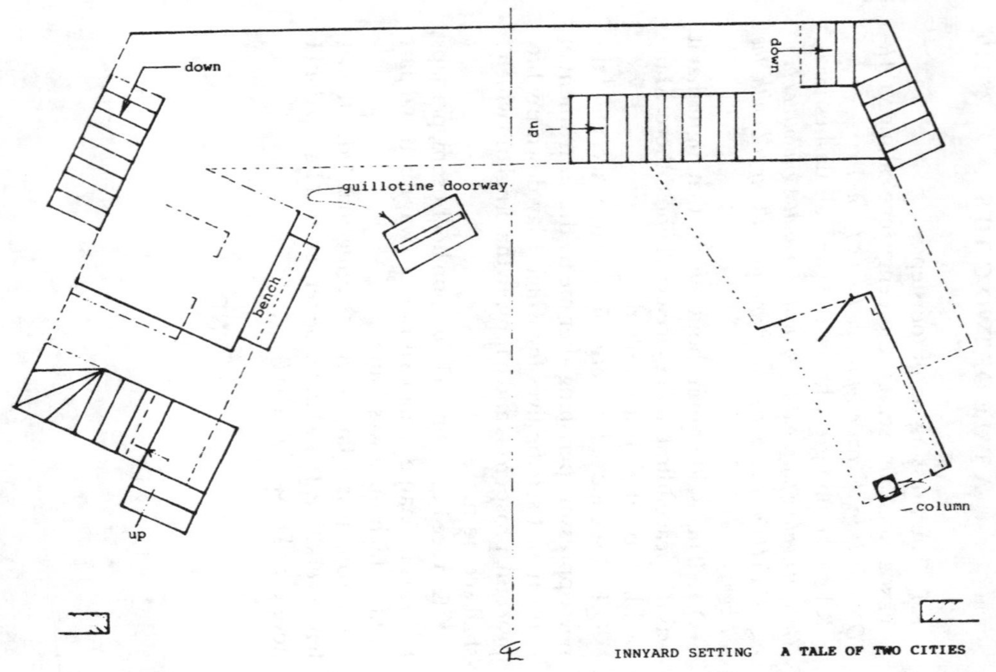

INNYARD SETTING A TALE OF TWO CITIES

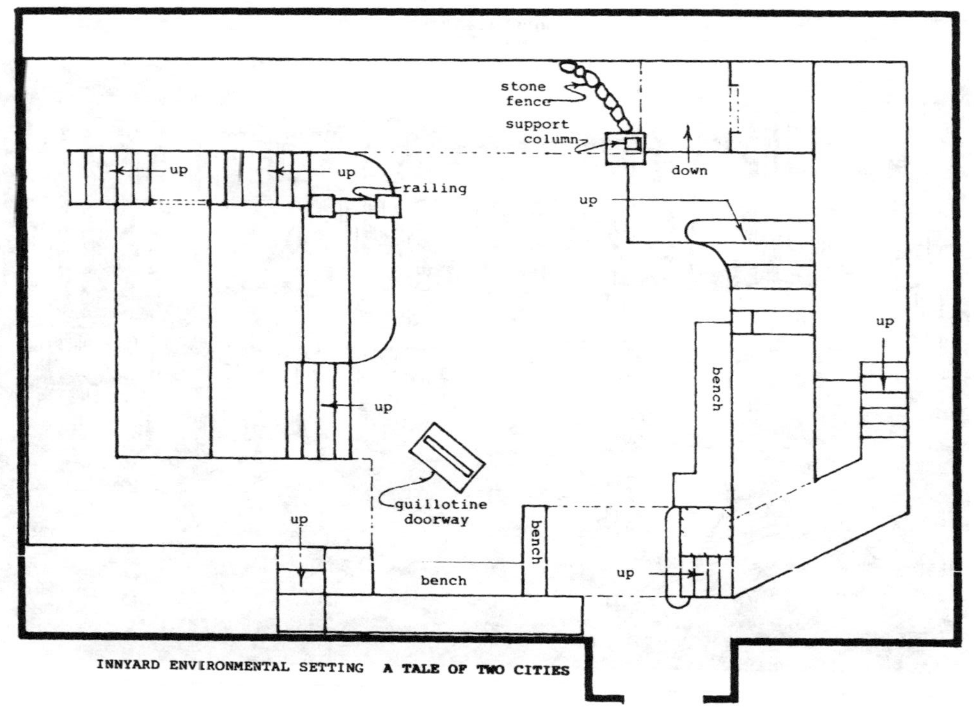

INNYARD ENVIRONMENTAL SETTING   A TALE OF TWO CITIES

SET DESIGN
A TALE OF TWO CITIES